Sweet Little Shamrock

By BIRDYE L. HARTLAND

Part 2 of the Shamrock Romances

Edited by Eva Valentine

Find all of the Shamrock Romances – and even more good old Victorian novels – on our <u>Tumblr</u> page!

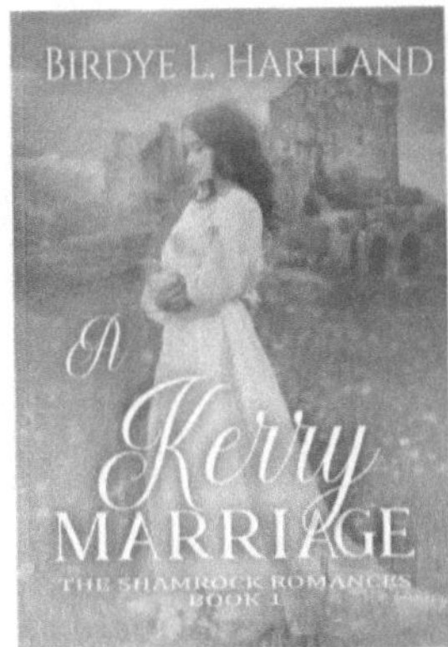
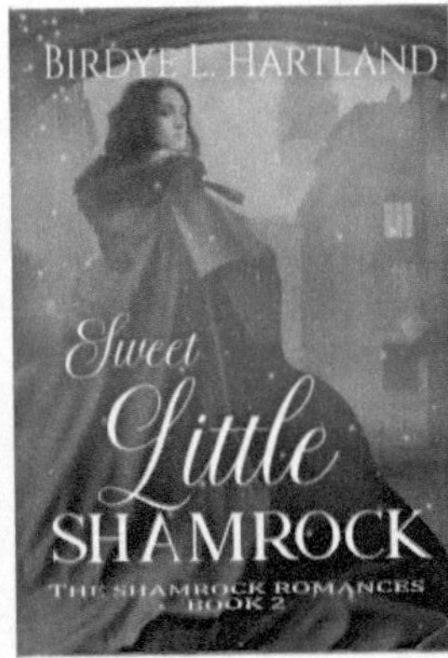
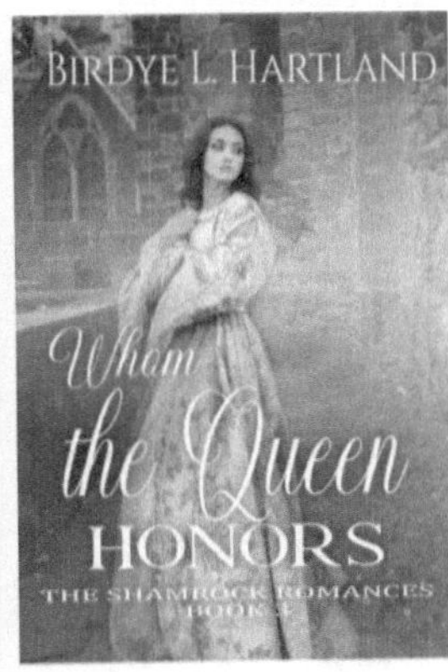

Grab the entire series today!
Book 1: A Kerry Marriage
Book 2: Sweet Little Shamrock
Book 3: Whom the Queen Honors

Heat level: No heat, sweet and clean

This is the Shamrock Romances series -- the first series being released by Victorian Workhouse Press. We are a tiny press dedicated to bringing back the old Victorian penny novels and polishing them until they're sparkling bright for today's readers.
Some people enjoy refurbishing old furniture; we love refurbishing old books.

Table of Contents

Editor's Note

Sweet Little Shamrock, as well as all the other books in this series, was originally published in 1900 as a penny novel. This was a type of serialized novel that was published weekly in a cheap paper that cost, of course, only a penny. These serialized novels came to be called penny dreadfuls because, in some of them, the quality of the writing was just ... dreadful. But some of these little stories were pretty good – and the readers at the time loved them.

I am a sucker for old books. When I was in high school, I read Victorian novels by the truckload. I got started on an old copy of *St. Elmo* that my grandpa had picked up at an auction, and read some of my books that my great-grandma had (I still have her old copy of *The Masquerader* by Katherine Cecil Thurston), and picked up many more via interlibrary loan. It's a love that still continues today.

I've been writing books for a long time, but I also love finding old books and editing them to bring them to a new audience. That's what I'm doing with these old penny novels. I'm transcribing them and editing them to bring them to the readers once more. These old stories are in the public domain, no longer under copyright, so anybody can do what they like with these old stories.

On one hand, it would be a lot easier to simply throw these little books out into the world, the way a lot of internet marketers are doing with books in the public domain. There are half a million (this is a very rough estimate) copies of *Pride and Prejudice* or *Anne of Green Gables* showing up on Amazon *every single day*.

A lot of internet marketers, looking for passive income, will grab a copy of some public domain book off Gutenberg, convert it into an ebook, and start selling it on Amazon.

I'm publishing these little books because I love those old Victorian books, and bringing these old books back to life is something of a fun craft project for me. I see stuff in the text that needs to be fixed, and I start fixing it, and the next thing I know, hours have passed and I'm sharpening the character motivation in Chapter IX. I spend hours cleaning up the text, which is a mess. Then I search for illustrations, format the book, proofread the pages, and get a pretty cover for it.

Pretty soon I have a tidy little book with a good story in it, ready to go, and I get a hiccup of pride. Look at that! I've rescued another little gem from the ash heap of history! It's a good feeling.

Some people enjoy restoring old furniture. We love restoring old books.

General Notes on Editing

Fond she was of the inverted style of sentence, so common in Victorian writing. "Well she knew no sympathy had he for all her misery" is one example of this style of recursive writing which pervaded this story. Well would it be wise for me to add that this style was not a grave fault in those days.

Things have changed! These days, authors and readers prize simple sentences that cut quickly to the heart of the matter, instead of these sweet convolutions. The Victorian style called for a gentler, more flowery style of writing, which lend a grand, sonorous sound to the words, and make every moment seem epic.

Victorian readers also loved what today's writers would sneeringly call *sentimentality* – the teary-eyed, beautiful heroine struggling against a cruel world that did not understand her secret heart, that maligned her even as she strove to stay pure-hearted, raising her eyes to God, who alone heard her secret prayers.

While editing this book, I straightened some sentences that needed it. Our dear author (or perhaps her editor) apparently had a comma gun that they'd shoot at random into the text, because I must have excised half a million commas out of this book. British Victorian style also uses semicolons heavily; I removed them and tidied up the sentences if they weren't necessary.

I also added a great deal of text to heighten the tension, or to continue plot elements that the author dropped, or to add some details or a few lines to better explain the characters' motivations. I also added period details, reading old newspaper articles to understand the role that Ireland played in the South Boer War (though I have Opinions about the lousy role that the English played in colonizing South Africa).

I also added in a little bit about the attack that Charlie wrote about in one of his letters, because when I was reading the original text, I was so aghast at this boneheaded move by the British generals, to fling thousands of their troops into the cannon's mouth in this way, that I had to ascertain that it was true.

Seeking Information About Birdye L. Hartland!

I have been trying to find out anything about Birdye Latham Hartland, the woman who originally wrote these stories, but to no avail. I've searched the British Library, Google Books, Ancestry, FamilySearch, Google, Newspapers.com, and other sites, using different variants of Birdye's name and switching up searches. I thought that, because she had these stories published, that I would at least pull up a few hits. To my complete surprise, there has been nothing.

Now, I've done genealogical research and historical research with some hard-to-track women, and generally I've been able to find at least a few nuggets of information about them through one of these methods. I'm a little dismayed that I have not had any luck.

What's more surprising, to me, is that when you have a name with a unique spelling, such as Birdye, it's more likely to come up on genealogical sites. Not in this case!

I will keep searching for Birdye, even after I publish these books. Birdye deserves to have some credit for her work all these years later.

If any of you readers have any information about poor Birdye, do please send it along to me at victorianworkhousepress@gmail.com. No bit of information is too small, I promise. You'd be surprised how a seemingly inconsequential piece of information can turn into a full-blown lead in genealogy! I'll do the follow-up research and pop it directly into these books.

Anyway, I hope you enjoy this book. I plan to release these serials monthly, so follow me on Twitter at @VictorianReader and on Tumblr!

Be sure to buy these books, and tell your friends to buy them too, because at this time I am locked in a freezing garret in some Victorian slum by an evil taskmaster and I'm not allowed to come out until I've published about 56 of these books. Send bread!

All best wishes,
Eva Valentine, editor
Victorian Workhouse Press

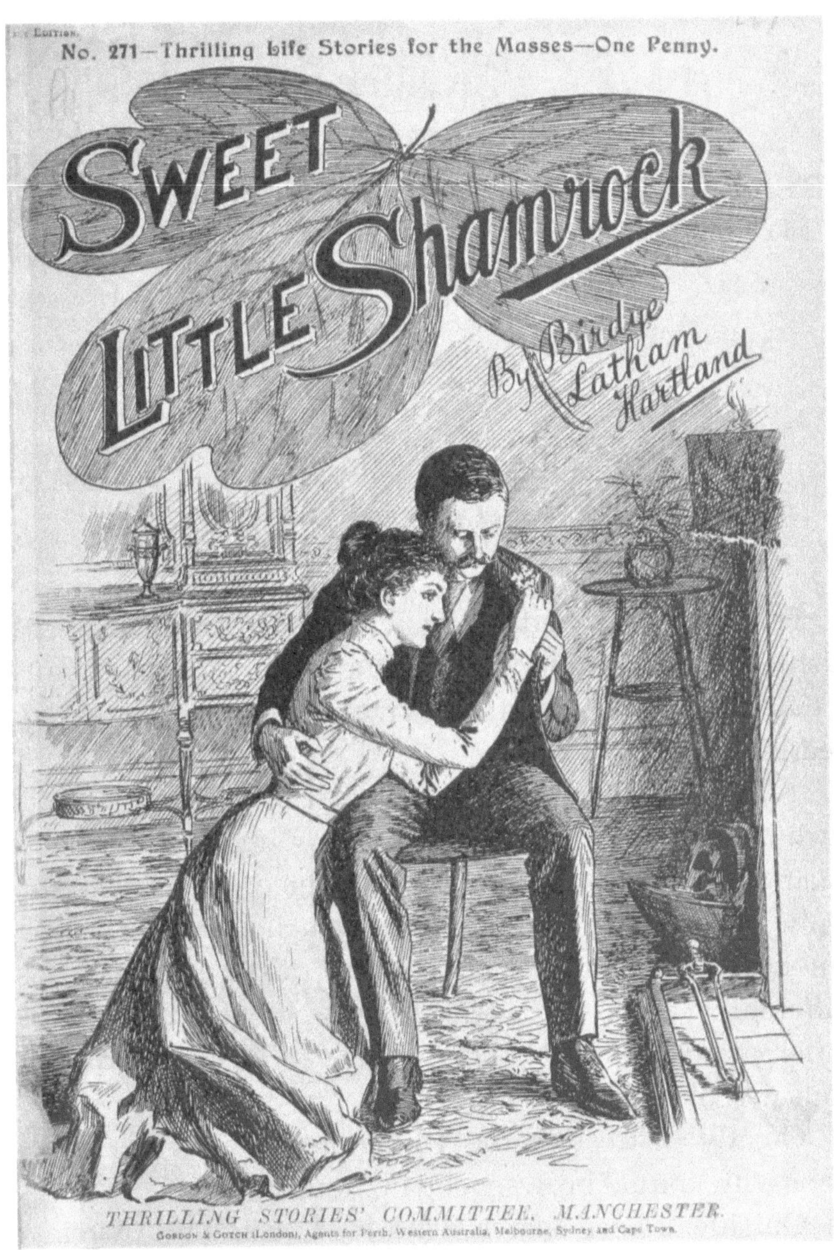
No. 271—Thrilling Life Stories for the Masses—One Penny.
SWEET Little Shamrock
By Birdye Latham Hartland
THRILLING STORIES' COMMITTEE, MANCHESTER.
Gordon & Gotch (London), Agents for Perth, Western Australia, Melbourne, Sydney and Cape Town.

Sweet Little Shamrock.

BY BIRDYE LATHAM HARTLAND, AUTHORESS OF "MY SHABBY DRESS," "OF ROYAL LINEAGE," "FAR ABOVE RUBIES," ETC, ETC.

CHAPTER I

HUGH SMITH had left his wife that morning in a very disturbed state of mind. His mother's many pointed hints – that Dewla was secretly in love with her cousin –were bearing fruit.

"Why should a mere cousin's welfare cause Dewla such great distress?" Hugh asked himself again and again, until the question seemed riveted upon his brain. Only once before had he seen her display such deep emotion, at the time of her father's death. But that was different. Surely, a parent would stand in a totally different relationship to a cousin – moreover, a distant cousin, too!

Greatly distressed, the young man paced his office floor with knitted brows, deep in thought.

Outside, a keen March wind blew, cold and piercing. Through the screened windowpanes, he could see the pedestrians hurriedly passing, eager to escape the chilling blast. Never before had the world seemed so cold and miserable. Mechanically he turned towards the fire and poked it into a brighter blaze.

Yet as the day wore on, the remembrance of Dewla's pale face, beautiful in its marble pallor, haunted him.

"What if she should be really ill?" became now the anxious thought uppermost in his mind. More than once he consulted his watch, chafing because today, unfortunately, he could not leave early. A business engagement occupied him, detaining him until the usual hour for returning home.

He had never felt the hours drag so heavily before; they seemed to run on leaden wheels. With all the impatience of a schoolboy, he watched the clock ticking ponderously toward quitting time.

When the clock chimed at last, Hugh, with great relief, picked up his hat. A moment later, he was hastening home with all possible speed like one set free. As he walked, he battled bravely with the keen east wind, almost unconscious of its strength, so engrossed was he with his own thoughts.

"Poor little Dewla! How had she spent the day?" Should he find her resting still, as he had bade her?

Musing thus, he hurried on until he reached the imposing entrance to Trafalgar House. Fumbling for his latchkey, he let himself in and strode immediately in the direction of Dewla's room – but to his astonishment and great concern, she was not there.

He stepped within. The fire had burnt low, all was still, and it was evident she had not been there for some time.

"My little dear," he said to himself. "Oh, Dewla, what happened to you?"

More quickly now, he descended the softly-carpeted stairs, and entered, without hesitation, the warmly lit drawing-room, expecting to find his wife here. Impatiently he glanced at the small group – she was not among them.

"Where is Dewla?" he inquired in tones of surprise, looking from his mother to his three sisters.

Mrs. Jonathan laughed. It was an uncomfortable sound at all times, but doubly so just now. He certainly didn't see anything amusing at the moment.

"She has gone for sympathy to her bosom-friend, Mrs. Wardell," returned Etta, laying aside her work.

"But I left her ill!" answered Hugh shortly.

"She seemed 'fit' enough, going off," declared Mrs. Jonathan. "I begged of her not to go, but all to no purpose. It was getting dark, too, but she openly disregarded my wishes." The great lady folded her arms with the air of a tragedy queen, surveying her son with an utter hopelessness of expression.

Hugh frowned. "Whatever takes her to Mrs. Warden's so frequently?" he inquired jealously.

"Working for the soldiers," Mabel sniffed. "I wondered what made Dewla so desperately in earnest over those flannel shirts – couldn't make it out for the life of me! Now, 'tis all explained beautifully. Why, she did it all for the sake of that cousin of hers – Charlie Cooke!"

Hugh glared at his sister almost savagely. "Don't be a fool, Mabel," he said hoarsely.

"My dear son," remonstrated Mrs. Jonathan. "Calm down."

The young man listened in silence, then took a turn up and down the room.

"I think," continued Mrs. Jonathan, in the same even tones, "that Dewla wronged you deeply when she accepted you as her husband."

At this he turned upon her. "She had no voice at all in the matter except to obey her father's dying wish. In that she was perfectly innocent."

Mrs. Jonathan could not conceal a sneer. Moreover, his loyalty annoyed her not a little.

"If a woman loves another man, she knows it well enough," she replied. "Therefore, it was wrong – very wrong – of her to force you to marry her!"

Hugh turned aside his face. It was growing white and stern, but Mrs. Jonathan was not going to spare him now. Her old grudge against her son, for marrying in haste, still rankled in her breast.

"Anyone with half an eye could see that she was in love with this Charlie," she went on. "Just watch her face as she talks of him. Why, it lights up in an instant, and she is another being altogether. Surely, you must have remarked all this for yourself, my son?"

Hugh almost writhed beneath her withering glance. Alas, it was true. He, too, had noticed it of late, but even to himself he scarce would admit such a thing.

"I dare say," put in his sister Mabel maliciously, "that Dewla has blabbed out all her sorrows into Mrs. Warden's open ears. And we all know that Mrs. Wardell is rather given to talking."

"Dewla is certainly very often invited there, and always without us," observed Margaret slowly.

"Why, of course," laughed Mabel, admiring the embroidered toe of her new slipper resting upon the fender – a more important matter in her eyes, than either Dewla or her troubles.

"My dear Hugh," said Mrs. Jonathan solemnly, "it was a terrible mistake – this trumped-up marriage, done all in a minute, so to speak. Why, it makes me sick to think of it."

Her son bent his head. "Don't! Mother," he cried, with deep earnestness. "Don't speak like that. I cannot bear it – because I love Dewla – love her with all my heart."

The great lady knit her brows angrily. She was not easily touched, and this declaration of affection on Hugh's part made her all the more bitter against Dewla.

"Look at how you're acting," she snapped, waving an imperious hand at Hugh. "It is this very love of yours which is blinding your eyes to her faults and failings. And well she knows it, too! She triumphs in the fact."

"You mistake my wife. She does not triumph in anything."

"Wife, pooh!" the great lady sputtered. "Her heart is not with you – it never was! That cousin, Charlie, whose name she continually flaunts in our faces, is a thousand times more to her than *you* are – though, indeed, you be her husband."

"You cannot say such things about Dewla," Hugh said.

"Yes, she can," Mabel sniffed, jabbing her needle into her embroidery. "We are trapped with that girl every day while you are at the office. I think we know her better than you do."

Mrs. Jonathan smiled and petted her daughter's hair as if she were a spaniel. "Well spoken, Mabel. You would do well to heed our warnings regarding that girl." Mabel smiled grandly.

A dull red color blazed on Hugh's cheek. His eyes flashed, but he spoke no word in return.

Hugh's mother shook her head, turning toward the fire. "Oh, do try and hide your too-evident devotion. A little severity on your part would bring Dewla to her senses, and make your love of more value in her eyes. At present, she takes it all as a matter of course."

Again he answered nothing. Standing there, stroking his moustache roughly, he presented a strange picture to those who had known him long.

Now his mother spoke in a coaxing tone of voice. "Etta is going to spend the evening with the Sedleys. Bella particularly requested that you might come, too." Bella's name rolled off her tongue as if it had been dipped in caramel. "I wish you would go and see her, Hugh."

But he only turned from her abruptly.

"Do come, Hughie," pleaded Etta. "It will seem like old times again. Dewla is out, and cannot possibly miss you. And I want an escort, you know."

"But Dewla – how is she to get home?" he demanded.

"I can send Duncan," his mother said shortly. "It is only a short walk, and Dewla loves anything in the way of outdoor exercise – it comes of her low country breeding, I suppose."

"She must not return on foot," answered Hugh, with unusual decision. "It is wild and bitterly cold. Send the carriage, mother. She was not well this morning." And his face softened as he recalled the memory of his young wife's pale, beautiful features when he had carried her upstairs, holding her close in his arms.

Mrs. Jonathan shrugged her shoulders wrathfully; he was still inclined to make too much fuss over Dewla. However, for the present, she must give way, and besides, it meant a great victory, his going to the Sedleys. She had won so far.

Before starting, Hugh talked to his mother again, reminding her that the carriage must be sent at a certain time, for Dewla still clung to her habits of early hours – a very plebian failing, in the great lady's eyes.

"The boy is a perfect fool about her," declared Mrs. Jonathan to her eldest daughter, once he'd left and they were alone. "It nearly drives me wild to see him behaving so. Oh, if only I could have foreseen what this trip to Ireland meant!"

"But," remonstrated Margaret, who liked occasionally to disagree with "the mater" for the sake of argument, "I think Dewla is equally attached to him."

Mrs. Jonathan gave her daughter a quick look of deep displeasure.

"Pooh! You think nothing of the kind," she returned flatly. "The girl has no affection for anyone, save that soldier! Hugh's love is just wasted on her. What a worthless, ungrateful thing she is. Would that I had never seen her!"

"We all wish that," retorted Mabel readily. "I, for my part, can't imagine why people rave about her beauty. She has nothing so wonderful to boast of. I could have shaken old Mrs. De Vere, when I heard her holding forth to Hugh about his young wife's rare loveliness. And he believed it all, I know, for he looked as proud as Punch!"

"Mrs. De Vere's son evidently thinks likewise," responded the elder sister, tossing back her black fringe impatiently. "He stares at Dewla by the hour. I've watched him more than once. He has no eyes now for Etta, or anyone else."

"Ugh! Don't be absurd," said Mrs. Jonathan crossly. "I rarely see Mr. De Vere even talking to Dewla! I am sure you are grossly mistaken, Margaret. Men, of course, naturally like a new face, and Dewla's uncommon accent is perhaps a little attractive to English ears."

"Yet she talks so little, especially of late," returned Etta slowly. "I used to rather like the funny way she said things, using peculiar words and phrases. I quite miss it all now, when she remains so silent."

Mrs. Jonathan shook out her ample silken skirts, with a gesture of impatience. "What next will you say, I wonder?" she demanded, rising from her comfortable chair with an impatient gesture.

CHAPTER II

WHEN the carriage drew up at Trafalgar House, Dewla alighted, then walked slowly up the white stone steps, an anxious expression in her wistful brown eyes. Would her dear Hugh be there to greet her? How she longed to see him smiling down into her eyes.

But when she entered, there was only Mrs. Jonathan, looking disgusted – the kind of look that one would give to a dog who had dragged a dead rat into the house.

"Well," was her mother-in-law's snooty greeting, "so you've come back."

"Yes, I have," Dewla replied, feeling as if the air had been knocked quite out of her reply. She turned her eyes to the floor, conscious that her return was hailed with neither pleasure nor delight. It was extremely painful to feel that no one wanted and watched for her coming. Hugh had always met her with a smile. But where was he tonight?

With a little sigh she went to the parlor and sat down with the rest of the girls. None of them troubled themselves with looking up from their conversation or taking any notice of her whatsoever. She may as well have been a ghost.

Dewla half-wished that she were.

Folding her hands together, Dewla gazed into the glowing firelight. Soon her thoughts were far away, and she was back again in the old days at Claisín. Oh! How happy they had been – her father, Charlie, and herself – together. The days were never long or dull, and the evenings always bright and merry.

How well she could see her dear old home – the long, oak paneled sitting-room; the shaded lamp that cast a happy glow, beside which her father's chair was drawn. She remembered how he loved to read to them from his favorite books. Charlie, busy with his tools, would be making some pretty knick-knack to adorn her room. She, plying her needle with a lazy kind of interest, listened to her father's melodic words all the while in happy contentment. Oh, how happy she had been.

And now – now the contrast!

"Are you asleep, child?" Mrs. Jonathan's braying voice broke in upon her long reverie.

Dewla started to her feet. Margaret snorted.

"There! You needn't look so scared – as though you'd seen a ghost," Mrs. Jonathan sneered, a corner of her mouth quirking up into a scornful smile. "But it is late. I thought you liked waking up at early hours – you are always *saying* so, at least."

With this parting shot, the great lady swept from the room, her skirts rustling like winter's blast among the dry, discolored leaves.

Dewla followed her mother-in-law at a little distance, going slowly up the wide staircase. She had never felt so alone in her whole life.

Dismissing her maid, Dewla drew a low seat close to the fire. She knew she would not be able to sleep, for she felt too miserable.

Taking her mother's Bible, she turned the pages over with tender, reverent fingers. Little pencil-marks met her at every glance, showing that her mother had read and loved it well.

She tried to read through it, but her head ached, and the misery that gnawed at her heart made it impossible to focus on the words on the page.

Clasping her hands together once more that day, Dewla prayed for her far-off cousin.

So engrossed was she that she did not hear her husband's approaching step upon the threshold of her room.

Hugh paused in surprise at finding her thus. How fair Dewla looked, like a spirit from another world in her trailing, white, loose robe, pleading thus, with upturned face, unconscious of his presence.

As though spellbound and rooted to the spot, he stood gazing upon her kneeling figure. He had seen a picture such as this, once, but he could not recollect just then when or where, only the picture was not so pure and fair as she.

And as he lingered thus, unnoticed in the deep shadow of the doorway, a faint sound fell from her quivering lips.

Listening with bated breath, he caught the murmur of her voice. Then, straining his ears, he heard the burden of her prayer.

Rooted to the spot, he gazed upon her kneeling figure.

"Lord, spare his dear life; make him well again. Oh, please cover him with your wings, my cousin, Charlie."

It was enough. The unseen listener withdrew softly and closed the door again. His face had lost its softened expression; now it was cold and stern.

"Mater is right," he muttered to himself. "She thinks of this Charlie at all times, and only of him."

Poking the dying fire in the study grate to a blaze, Hugh flung himself moodily into a chair and picked up the nearest book to hand, then lit a cigar. There was no one to disturb him here.

The pages of his volume proved altogether unsatisfactory. Closing the book with an impatient bang, he tossed it aside. Leaning his face upon his folded arms, he gave himself up entirely to the strange thoughts which chased each other through his excited brain.

Was it true that the fair girl that he had made his wife, loved another man. Was it true that he was nothing to her except in name? Covering his face with his hands, he groaned aloud.

How sweet the near past seemed now – but now its sweetness was gone forever, leaving only a dreary future.

Dewla had meant so much to him in those first months of their married life. He had thought – fool that he was – that she was beginning to love him, even as he loved her. How blind he was! What an utter fool!

With a twinge of pain, he remembered the many tales about "Cousin Charlie" she was always telling him. How the two of them used to boat together on the lake, while her cousin amused her with long tales of country folklore about which the district abounded.

Hugh had suspected nothing. He thought it was only natural that she should talk much of one with whom she had grown up with all a sister's intimacy.

He had been slow, indeed, to believe his mother's suggestions. But now, tonight, all doubts were swept from his mind, as he saw with his own eyes Dewla's tears, and heard the words which fell from her lips.

CHAPTER III

AS the days went by, the rift between Dewla and her husband widened, and gradually they drifted further and further apart. Dewla's gentle heart pondered over the change, so little at first, now great indeed.

"What have I done?" In vain she took herself severely to task. In word and deed, surely she had striven hard to please. She often shed hot, scalding tears when she was alone, tears seen by none save He "who knoweth our thoughts afar off," and "seeth in secret."

One evening, Hugh came home with some news. "Have you heard?" he asked at the table that night, as his family and their guests enjoyed a sumptuous dinner. "The Queen intends to pay a visit to Ireland early next month!"

Dewla's whole face lit up with pleasure. She nearly dropped her fork in the joy she felt at such an unexpected announcement. "The Queen? In my dear country?"

"Oh, it is only some wild report." Naturally, it was Mrs. Jonathan who spoke. She was sitting at the end of the long dining-table, resplendent in satin, gay ribbons, and lace. "One never can believe such statements, especially just now, in the time of war."

Mabel snorted. "Why, it would be almost safer to face the Boers at once, than venture among the wild Irish!" she declared, with a suggestive glance towards her sister-in-law.

Dewla bent her head over her plate, cutting her mutton into tinier and tinier pieces so she wouldn't have to look up.

"The Queen is pleased with the splendid bravery of her Irish soldiers," observed Mr. De Vere, who was dining also at Trafalgar House, and had noticed Mabel's pointed look. "Why, they've done magnificent work in South Africa. I don't wonder that Mrs. Hugh is proud of her countrymen – and well she might be, too," he added kindly. "They've most certainly proved themselves the bravest of the brave."

Dewla gave him a look full of gratitude. He bowed slightly, feeling amply repaid.

"The Queen will *never* go there," proclaimed Mabel, "especially at this time of year. I always imagine Ireland a great, big, uninteresting bog, with shamrocks growing over it."

"I believe the little green shamrock is indigenous to Erin's Isle, is it not?" Mr. De Vere asked Dewla. "My mother has had roots sent to her, time after time, but all to no purpose – they will not thrive in English soil! It seems strange, considering that the climate is so much the same."

Dewla shook her head. "It is very different in this country, I think," she said impulsively. "Why, it seems always sunless and smoky here, while in Ireland we have no smoke, and all sunshine."

Mrs. Jonathan laughed scornfully. "I wonder," she said with heightened color in her face, "that you made the exchange from sun to smoke!"

Dewla shot a helpless look at her husband, but Hugh was engaged in conversation with one of the guests, and did not hear his mother's remark from his end of the long, flower-decked table.

"I suppose you know," remarked De Vere, again addressing himself to Dewla, "that Her Majesty has granted permission for all her soldiers to wear the sprig of shamrock this Patrick's Day."

"Oh, has she? I am so glad. But Charlie won't have any, I am afraid, so far away in Africa. And besides, he is wounded now – dangerously wounded." Dewla's lips quivered painfully at the thought.

Now Hugh heard, and he watched her face as she spoke. Even from here, he could see the glitter of tears upon her downcast lashes. Though her tears touched him, he felt sore at heart, for the very mention of her cousin's name was hateful to his ears.

It was De Vere who came to the rescue, with kindly thoughtfulness, anxious to divert her attention. "Will you not tell us something of this wonderful St. Patrick, Mrs. Hugh, and his time-famed shamrock? I confess to be most woefully ignorant, and need enlightenment badly. For instance, how did such a humble weed – I hope I am not irreverent – come to be the national emblem of Ireland?"

Dewla shook away the tears and regarded him in wondering surprise. "Do you really not know?" she inquired incredulously.

He, laughing, shook his head, and tried to appear penitent, but he looked so funny that Dewla smiled. "When St. Patrick came to Ireland first—"

"Why, I thought the great saint *grew* there, along with the 'sweet little shamrock.'"

"Oh, Mr. De Vere, you funny man! St. Patrick came to Ireland in the fifth century in a boat, and from the day he set foot on the Isle of the Pagans, his whole soul thirsted to make our nation into an Isle of Saints. He found poor Ireland in Pagan darkness, and when he left, she was entirely Christian. Surely, such a transformation was never witnessed in the world's history!"

Dewla had been so carried away by the enthusiasm of her favorite theme that she quite forgot herself. She had been perfectly unconscious of her mother-in-law's withering glances the whole time she'd been speaking.

"Really!" laughed the great lady, "you might pose as a platform speaker – a second Mrs. Chant. Is it the custom in Ireland for women to preach?"

Dewla bent her head, painfully conscious that everything she did was displeasing to those of Trafalgar House.

"I am very grateful, indeed, for such valuable information," answered De Vere quickly, and, even at the cost of offending his hostess, continued. "But you have not answered my question about the shamrock, and I am most curious to learn all I can."

"Pray wait until dinner is concluded," commanded the great lady stiffly. "You and Dewla will have ample time then for exchanging ideas."

Despite Mrs. Jonathan's injunction, hurled as if from On High, De Vere was not to be baffled. After dinner, having joined the ladies in the drawing-room, he made his way directly to Dewla's corner.

Etta tried to snare him as he passed, saying, "Come and talk to me. I promise not to bore you with long soliloquies like *some* people." Mr. De Vere merely nodded in a friendly manner to Etta and kept moving.

Dewla was alone in her corner, slowly drinking her coffee, her eyes fixed dreamily upon a beautiful picture hanging upon the wall. The exquisite paintings which adorned the rooms pleased her most of all the costly surroundings of Trafalgar House. She was so lost in contemplation of the painting that she failed to notice the young man's noiseless approach.

"I have come for more enlightenment," he said in playful tones as he took a chair near her own.

She turned her beautiful dark eyes full upon him in questioning appeal.

"Do you really care about my native land?" she asked wistfully.

"Most certainly. Why should you doubt my sincerity?"

"Because so few English take any interest in poor, neglected Ireland."

Mr. De Vere leaned forward in a winning manner. "Excuse me, Mrs. Hugh. In this you are entirely wrong. At the present moment, it seems to me your country is the most favored spot of the empire. With Royal patronage smiling upon it, and the Queen preparing a royal visit to your emerald nation, what more can we English do to atone for the dark past? We are showing our admiration and sympathy for the brave, heroic soldiers who faced death so fearlessly in the cause of justice and right. Today, if I could be Irish, I would!"

A smile flitted over Dewla's face. Such words were new and so very sweet to her ears.

"I was brought up to so love my native land, so it pains me to hear it lightly spoken of," she said softly. "Besides, the happiest days of all my life were spent there."

She spoke the last words so sadly, that De Vere looked away. He could not bear the pensive droop of the sweet, sensitive mouth.

"Tell me the rest of St. Patrick's history, please," he suggested, anxious once again to divert her thoughts from painful reflection. "That is, of course, if you care to."

"Oh, I love talking of anything that pertains to Ireland," she answered brightly. "It is so seldom I can find anyone willing to listen. You are giving me a treat, I assure you."

"Then we are debtors one to the other," he retorted, laughing. He liked to see sunshine stealing into his companion's face, chasing the clouds of sadness away. To hear his hostess talk to Dewla, he strongly suspected that the young lady was seldom treated to sunshine or laughter. "After all in every land, St. Patrick is revered as a fit type of the highest sanctity."

"Perhaps so, but in Ireland, his memory is almost worshipped. Tradition says that when he lit his Easter fire on the eve of his first sermon, a Druid exclaimed that if it were not quickly extinguished, it would burn for all ages in the land. The exclamation of that Pagan priest seemed really a prophecy, because the fire of faith then kindled in Irish hearts will never be extinguished. Ever since that first sermon preached upon the hilltop, Erin's little shamrock has become dear to all her children. It is the emblem of faith and nationality. St. Patrick, finding his hearers so unlearned, plucked it from the green sod at his feet to explain to them the wonderful mystery of the Holy Trinity.

"Imagine that sight on Tara's Hill, where some of the greatest chieftains were assembled there that day. Never, perhaps, did human teacher choose a more fitting token, thus revealing expressively the wonderful unity of the Godhead. So dear did this little shamrock become to a grateful nation, that, in after days, it adorned the crowns of Ireland's Kings for three centuries of peace, when learning and sanctity flourished together in the land.

"When, at length, cruel war – ah! it is ever cruel! – came, the shamrock shone on her victorious banners in many a hard-fought battle, and once more it shone again as the emblem of glory, when the nation was allowed to breathe for a while in peace."

Dewla felt a little shy all of a sudden, having talked for so long, and her voice died away.

"Pray continue," Mr. De Vere pleaded, glancing at Mrs. Jonathan, who was too busy talking with her guests to notice Dewla and needle her. "It is a pleasure to hear your history."

Dewla smiled shyly, but continued. "Yes, the dear little shamrock was Ireland's comfort in her long night of sorrow. Full many a time it was trampled in the earth, bedewed with the best and bravest blood in the land, but, like the faith which it represented, it is undying. Famine, pestilence, and the sword mowed down my people, but 'the dear little shamrock,' budding forth on St. Patrick's Day, spoke of the faith and nationality which never dies. The heartbroken emigrant, bidding good-bye to kith and kin, and the land of his love, reverently plucks the little green weed, and, dropping a tear upon it, presses it to his heart to accompany him in his weary exile.

"Other nations were blessed with illustrious teachers, and their soil was crimsoned with the blood of martyrs, but in no land are they held in such reverence as St. Patrick is in Ireland. Wherever one of Irish blood can be found, at home or abroad, in the East and West, there they love the little shamrock. Ireland glories in the heroism of her sons, and the beauty of her daughters. When all seemed lost, and crushing defeat appeared certain, often Irish valor has won the day. Today, Irish missionaries are heralds of the gospel they love, in the most distant parts of the earth."

At this moment, Hugh came towards them with a passing remark to his friend, De Vere. The flush of enthusiasm seemed to fade suddenly from Dewla's face, and the flash of joy from her eyes.

"Your wife has been giving me such a glowing account of St. Patrick," said the guest of the evening. "I feel quite envious, because I am not altogether Irish."

Hugh laughed a funny sort of laugh.

"You should write a tale," continued De Vere, turning towards Dewla. "I am sure you could do it well."

"I often thought I'd love to try," she answered thoughtfully, "but perhaps it would not be worth publishing. You see, I am not highly educated as English girls are." She had been told this many times by Mrs. Jonathan and her daughters, until she had come to believe it herself.

"You seem to me to have been very well taught, Mrs. Hugh," returned De Vere earnestly. "I wish more girls had had such an education as yours."

Dewla locked up wonderingly. "I am afraid you do not understand," she answered gently. "I am not accomplished, and have no degrees to my name. The little I know, Father taught me himself, but he was a very clever man, and very deeply read."

"If you have finished your lecture, Dewla, or whatever you call it," cried Mrs. Jonathan from the background, "pray release poor Mr. De Vere. I am sure he is pining for a change of conversation. I did not know, before tonight, that you, in common with your countrymen, were possessed with the gift of the gab."

In vain the young man protested that he was very happy to listen to Dewla's words, but the hostess was not to be put off. Mrs. Jonathan marched him off in triumph.

CHAPTER IV

WHEN he was gone, leaving her alone again, Dewla sat a little apart, deep in thought. De Vere's words about writing a tale sank deeply into her mind.

Why should she not? She had lots of time – too much, in fact – and no one should know about it until it all appeared in print. And she would certainly not whisper a word of it to Mrs. Jonathan or the girls, for she knew they would trample it with their harsh judgements.

But would Hugh be pleased?

The very thought sent her pulses throbbing wildly.

Oh, if she could do something – something which should cause him to be proud of his little Irish wife – how glad she would feel, how unutterably thankful her heart would be. Any toil or trouble would seem as nothing, if such an end were gained.

Spurred by this new ambition, the desire grew upon her. So, while the rest of the party talked, she began there and then to weave a tale in her mind, one which would be transferred to paper on the morrow.

The following morning, the door had barely shut behind Hugh when, in feverish haste, Dewla collected her writing materials and hurried upstairs.

Carefully closing her door against all intruders, Dewla sat down gleefully before the fire, anxious to start the first page of her wonderful tale, the success of which she fondly hoped would help to win back her dear husband's love once more.

Hope and joy fluttered in her breast. Oh, if it should but succeed!

Clasping her hands together, she breathed forth an earnest prayer for help. Surely, it must be successful – this little plan of hers.

And this is the story she wrote:

SUNSHINE AND SHADOW

Is it not ever so?
Where shall we find
Light, that may cast
No shadow behind?
-- Frances Havergal.

"'Tis awfully hard to say good-bye, isn't it, Ruby?" Stanley Cleveland bent over his bride-wife with a look of deep tenderness. His departing train was nearly ready to leave, and he stood by the stairs, his merry brown eyes smiling into hers. "Why, I feel inclined to chuck this fishing trip altogether, and just tip the guard to toss my Gladstone bag out of the baggage car."

But Ruby shook her head. "The change will do you good," she said, loyally battling with her tears and endeavoring to speak gaily. "And a fortnight won't be so long in passing, will it?" Yet her lips quivered, despite her efforts to be brave.

The porter was slamming the doors ere Cleveland sprang into the train. Leaning over the closed door, Cleveland, despite all the spectators, touched his wife's soft cheek. "My beautiful wife. How I love you!"

Then the shrill whistle sounded, and the train moved slowly off.

"Write me a letter as soon as you get home!" he called, leaving Ruby standing upon the deserted platform, her eyes blinded with a rush of tears.

It was their first separation after five blissfully happy months of wedded life. An old friend of Stanley's had – after several fruitless attempts – finally persuaded him into a very reluctant promise to spend a few weeks with him on one of the Scotch lakes. But, at the moment of parting, he was sorely tempted into foregoing the engagement altogether. One little word from Ruby would have kept her husband at her side, but she, so unselfish in her great love, bade him go, though her heart yearned that he might stay. She hardly knew why she felt the parting so keenly.

"It is because of my Irish temperament," she thought, wiping the tears from her eyes, and struggling to dispel what she fancied was a mere superstition on her part.

Ruby's early girlhood had been spent in a very lonely, wild part of the county Kerry. Her father she did not remember, and her mother had died some two years before our story opens. A maiden aunt, living in London, immediately adopted the orphans, Ruby and her older brother Jervis.

Life in the great Metropolis was not altogether happy for Ruby. She sadly missed the rural beauty and freedom of her dear country home.

But a new era dawned upon her, from her first meeting with Stanley Cleveland. After a few short weeks they became engaged, and Ruby's heart awoke to the sweet, strong love of womanhood – a love which increased and grew once she became the happy bride of a true, good man.

Only one tiny speck clouded her fair sky of blue. Her brother had altered much since they had left their secluded home amid the blue Kerry mountains. Though she could not quite understand the change, it saddened her much.

Whilst living with him, Jervis had constantly taken her pocket money – always forgetting to return it. Only a short time after she had married, he started begging her for larger sums. Each time he promised never to incur debts again. Yet each time he would come back, having forgotten his earlier promises.

Ill at ease, she had told her husband, who appeared very displeased.

"You must never advance him money again, Ruby," he said sternly. "Jervis has more money than is good for him. Unfortunately, he has contracted gambling habits, and more than once I have talked plainly with him about it." But her husband did not like to grieve his proud, young wife. He couldn't bear to tell her that he, too, had helped her brother out of his difficulties.

Once her husband's train was out of sight, Mrs. Cleveland returned home alone, to find her beautiful mansion dismally lonely. A deserted air seemed to hang about everything. How she missed her husband at every turn – his step upon the stairs, or his merry whistle from the garden.

"Oh, what would life be now, without his love?" she thought. Shuddering at the bare suggestion, she clasped her hands together and silently prayed that God might bless and guard him.

Stanley Cleveland had been gone only twenty-four hours, yet the time appeared doubly long to his wife, who already began to count the days to his return. She was seated in her own pretty morning-room, a tender smile upon her face, for his letter lay before her, and she was just about to answer it. "It's the next best thing to seeing him," she thought as she took up her pen.

But, before she could write the first line, a quick step sounded on the corridor, the door burst open, and in came her brother Jervis.

She shrieked, startled, and her pen went flying.

"I knew I'd find you here," he said coolly, in answer to her surprise. "Heard Stanley was away, so thought I'd have a run down, and see how you were getting along."

"It was very kind of you," she answered, trying to calm her pounding heart, and attempting to banish the conviction that he had other motives for his visit.

"Beastly hot in town," he went on. "Stanley's a lucky dog to have this Oxford seat, and lots of tin to boot."

Ruby closed her mouth suddenly as a sense of dread came over her.

"Aunt Martha's rather in the fusses lately, so don't you tell her I've been here, nor Stanley either. But I suppose you can't help telling him, now, every little fiddle-faddle – wives always do."

The warm color rose to his sister's brow at his taunting tone, and she bit her lip.

"That's the worst of matrimony," he continued. "It robs one entirely of sisters. For I remember, Ruby, when you'd stand by a fellow and give him a helping hand, without publishing it abroad."

"What do you mean, Jervis?" She lifted her clear, steadfast eyes to his. "Have you forgotten the other instances where I have helped you many and many a time?"

The young man was silent for a moment as if she'd caught him out. Then, leaning his elbows on the table, he covered his face with his hands and groaned aloud.

"Jervis, what is the matter?" She sprang to her feet and knelt at his side. "Will you not tell me, dear?"

"Ruby," he muttered, in tones of despair. "I am ruined – ruined for life. If you do not help me now, it will be the last time, I swear."

"Come now, you say this every time to come to me for money."

His eyes narrowed, and she subsided. "This is my story," he said. "Deep in debt, I knew not what to do. Then the temptation came. I stole money from my boss's safe. If I don't replace that money by tomorrow night, I am done for."

He raised his haggard face, and saw that her beautiful eyes were filled with pity and grief.

"Oh! Jervis, how could you?" she gasped in deep distress.

With a gesture of impatience he turned from her. "I thought that you would have helped me," he cried bitterly. "I was a fool to believe you would!"

She looked at him in reproachful wonder. "How much?" she asked slowly.

"Five hundred pounds," he returned defiantly.

She swayed, shaken by the sum. "So much! Oh! Jervis, this is terrible. You mustn't do things like that," she cried in dismay.

"It wasn't my fault," he retorted hotly. "Besides, you or Stanley wouldn't mind such a trifle."

"That is not a trifle!"

"It's only a poor beggar like me that gets knocked over!"

"No, Jervis, I cannot come to your rescue every time you choose to make a terrible decision. Every time I help you, you promise it will be the last time. Instead, you lose larger and larger sums! And you still expect me to rescue you. How could you do such a thing, my brother?"

He saw the resolve in her face and went pale.

Then he turned away. "Fine, if that is how you want to be. Leave me to twist in the wind, my sweet sister! Anyway, if that money is not returned by tomorrow, I'll just save you the trouble and … and put a bullet through my head."

"Jervis!" Ruby clutched her heart. "I beg of you, do not do such a thing."

His eyes sharpened at her distress. "Aye, I would," he said as if he'd found his ace. "I would. I'd rather kill myself than stand the risk of transportation. Once they send me to Australia with all the other convicts, I'd never come back. Do you hear me?"

Ruby shivered. "What can I do, Jervis?" she asked piteously. "I have not half that amount with me, and Stanley will not return for perhaps a fortnight. I see no way in which I could help you."

But he, looking at her troubled eyes, took courage. "There is a way in which you can get the money, sis," he said quickly. "That is, if you really wish to help me out of this hole."

"Well?" she asked anxiously.

"There are money-lenders in London by the dozen who would advance all you want. Your husband's name – so well-known – would be guarantee enough."

Ruby shrank away, appalled.

He noticed the movement. "Pooh!" he cried, irritated. "I might have known you, and saved myself the trouble of coming."

"Jervis, this is wrong!" She could not help the tears starting to her eyes. "I am, indeed, willing to help you, but I cannot do this thing. It would not be honorable to my husband. If he were here, he would not do it."

Her brother grabbed her arm. "But sis, don't you see? He need never know. We can easily pay off the money without his knowledge."

"Yet you said something about his name?" she faltered.

"Oh, that's a mere matter of form," he returned eagerly. "I know a decent old chap – in fact, did business with him. So do lots of your nice, good people who live so high-and-mighty in these fine houses. This friend of mine would make everything square in a twinkle."

Ruby was silent, a conflict waging in her breast, but she drew herself up. "No," she said. "I am sorry, but I cannot do this thing."

"Of course, sis," he said. "Of course! If that's how it's going to be, then that's fine. If you'd rather see your only brother dead, why, it doesn't much matter, does it?" He sneered. "One shot, and it's all over! You needn't bother to put up a tombstone, mind – you can save your money there, too."

"Don't! Jervis," she pleaded in great distress, but he was not to be silenced.

"Perhaps it would be just as well to bury me beside mother, in the old Kerry churchyard. You and I used to gather daisies there once – they grew so big, in the long grass. We were happy then. There was no Stanley Cleveland to come between us, telling you what to do, and robbing me of my own sister's love."

"Jervis, you know that I love you still," she moaned. "It is cruel of you to talk thus."

"Well, 'tis no use wasting time," he said, rising. "My hours are numbered, so I must say good-bye, and it is forever this time, Ruby. I hope you won't reproach yourself when I'm dead."

She gasped, holding out a hand. "Give me a little time to think, Jervis," she pleaded, stopping him from walking to the front door. "Perhaps, tomorrow…"

"Pah! Tomorrow would be too late. If this is to be done at all, it must be today!"

Putting both hands to her face, she stood irresolute. "You mean—" she began.

He caught both her shoulders. "I mean that you must come to London, and talk to this money lender immediately. There is no time to waste," he said, glancing at the timepiece.

Still she hesitated, her breast heaving with conflicting emotions.

"Well, good-bye, Ruby. You can sometimes think of me when…"

"Stay, Jervis," she cried, with white, cold lips, feeling as if the words were wrenched out of her. "Enough. I will come with you. God will forgive me if I am doing wrong."

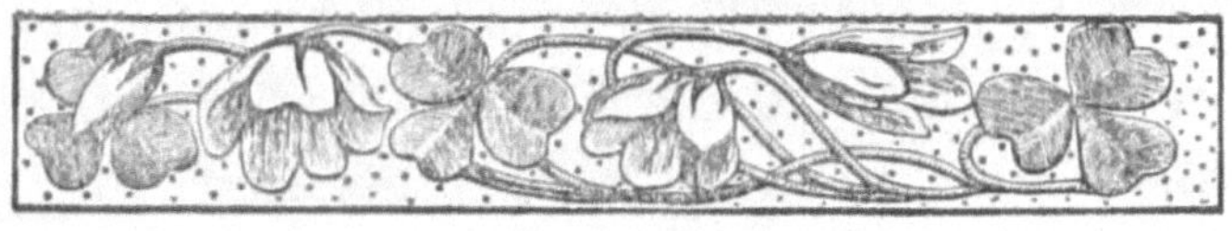

It was evening when she returned home, weary in body, and bearing a troubled, aching heart.

When she reached her room, she cried out. The post had already gone, and she had not replied to Stanley's tender, loving note. The letter she had started still lay upon the table, unfinished.

With a long, bitter moan, she flung herself upon a chair and wept bitterly. It was no use writing now. He could get it no sooner. Perhaps tomorrow she would feel better, and could finish her missive.

Instead, the following morning found Ruby Cleveland seated by her davenport, her face pale and sad, bearing visible traces of a long, sleepless night.

With pale, compressed lips, she took up her pen once more. Then she paused, for how was she to begin? What excuse can she offer for not having written sooner?

My dear, I have not been well ... but her pen did not move. Ruby could not dissemble, did not wish to write an untruth, but she was trying to write a letter that breathed love and cheer while this terrible deed she had done wrong blotted out both. She would have to lie to her husband to protect her brother.

Her heart rebuked her for holding any secret apart from her husband.

So what, then, should she do?

With a long-drawn sigh, she rested her aching brow upon her folded arms. Stanley had told her to give Jervis no more help. She had disobeyed his wishes outright – yea, worse. She had saved her brother from ruin, but at what cost?

A light tap upon the door bestirred her, and Bridget noiselessly entered. Bridget was her nurse from her old Irish home, who had come with her to her new home after Ruby had married.

"You said, ma'am," she began, pretending not to notice her tear-stained eyes, "as how you had a letter to send the master by early post."

Ruby started, and glanced at her watch. She had not realized how late it was. In desperation, she seized her pen and began to write some hurried lines, hardly knowing what she said.

A few minutes more, and the letter was dispatched. Still the young mistress of Cleveland Manor sat beside her desk, and to her lips she pressed the words her husband's hand had traced. Dearer to her heart was that scrap of paper, than the costliest jewels.

A week passed slowly by – the longest and most wretched that Ruby had ever known.

How she longed for – yet dreaded – her husband's return. Her stealthy visit to the money lender's office haunted her like a deadly nightmare. Her rounded cheeks were fast losing their bright glow, and her eyes were dimmed by tears.

Her letters to Stanley were short and constrained – so unlike those she had meant to send – for she found it impossible to write freely while this weight lay so heavy upon her heart. The tender words filling her breast found no expression, and failed to reach him.

But now she began to notice a very perceptible change in her husband's letters. Though she loved and treasured them, yet she was sorely conscious of a "something" lacking. They were growing shorter and colder.

Ruby had commissioned her faithful Bridget to sell some family trinkets that had been left to her by her mother. Though it cost her many tears to give up these beautiful items that her mother had once treasured, she did so. These had realized a large sum. With very mingled feelings, Jervis' sister posted the money to the lender, in partial payment of his loan.

One afternoon she was sitting in her luxurious drawing-room, an open book upon her knee, but her thoughts were far away. Suddenly she recognized a well-known step upon the stairs. She cried out in joy.

A moment more, and her husband – the subject of her daydream – came into the room to her, his handsome face lighting up to see her.

Trembling in every limb, she rose to meet him, something more than mere surprise robbing her of words.

"Well!" he cried, catching her to his breast. "Are you not glad to see me, little wife?"

She hid her burning face upon his shoulder.

"What! No welcome ready?" he asked, after a moment's silence.

She merely clutched him more tightly.

"Ruby," he continued, his voice strangely husky, "are you not glad to have me back, after all those long days of absence?"

She nodded. But a choking sensation in her throat seemed to stifle her happy words ere they reached her quivering lips.

"Ruby, Ruby, what does this mean?" he asked gravely. Lifting her reluctant face, he gazed into her shrinking eyes. Then his brow grew troubled, for he read something there which he had never seen in their tranquil depths before – an expression more of fear than love.

"Is there anything that you have to tell me, Ruby?" he asked. "Your letters were always so short. You said so little about yourself."

Still she was silent, with averted face, her chest heaving. She tried to speak, but she was so ashamed of herself that she could not force out a single word.

With a gesture of impatience, his arms about her drooping form relaxed their hold, and he turned away in displeasure. Then, in a voice unmistakably cool, he inquired about his letters, and quitted the room without another glance at his wife's face.

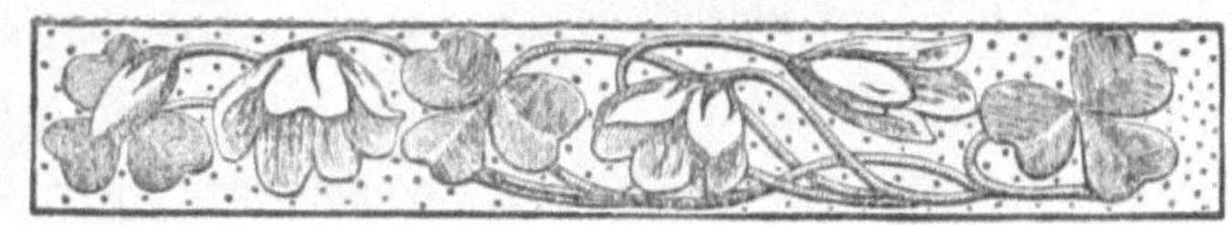

Perplexed, Cleveland trudged about through his home, his heart broken that his homecoming had turned out so badly. What had changed his beautiful Ruby? Her letters were now so short, and that was why he returned so soon; but he could not imagine what had happened to make her act this way, nor did it seem that she meant to enlighten him.

Evening brought with it no further explanation – Ruby was silent and sad. Her manner, which had puzzled him, now began to irritate him. Had she ceased to love him? The thought rankled in his mind. He strove to discover some clue to explain what had happened.

At the breakfast table, next morning, in looking through the contents of the letter bag, he came upon an envelope addressed to his wife in an unknown, masculine hand.

Passing it to her, he could not fail to notice the change which overspread Ruby's face. Nor did she attempt to break the seal – only thrust it hurriedly beneath her gown.

In awkward silence Stanley stood, expecting that she would surely now make some explanation. But no, she sat at the head of the table, pale and trembling, her eyes upon her plate, her lips closed.

That afternoon, Stanley Cleveland ran up to town, merely saying that he would spend some days at the club, and not return till the end of the week.

He received an enthusiastic reception from his old chums, who tried hard to persuade him into joining them in a Mediterranean cruise. At first, he felt almost inclined to go. They were starting in a few days, and he thought it would be a good way in which to punish Ruby. Yet his old love held him back.

Early one afternoon, he was leisurely strolling clown the Strand, conversing with a friend, who suddenly remarked, "Why do you hide your wife's peerless beauty away in the country? One never gets a glimpse of her now. It was quite by chance that I caught sight of her here about a week ago."

"You did? Where?" inquired Stanley.

"Why, in town, of course. She was driving with a very good-looking chap, too."

Cleveland was a man of wonderful self-control, yet he almost reeled as he listened. Here, at last, seemed some clue to Ruby's altered manner towards him. The next train found him whirling down towards Cloverdale.

Meanwhile, his pretty wife, all unconscious of the impending storm, was bending over a delicate piece of needlework, a smile so tender on her lips. A new, strange joy had stolen into her life, and its sweetness, for the time, seemed to banish all the gloomy shadows from her breast. How she longed for her husband's return. She wanted so to have him share her secret.

The evening breeze stole softly in through the open casement, and gently touched the stray, sun-kissed locks. How fair and sweet she looked with a soft flush upon her dimpled cheeks.

For a moment Stanley paused upon the threshold of her room, and as he gazed upon the pleasant home picture, his face softened.

Looking up, Ruby uttered a glad cry of joy, and rose quickly, dropping the dainty work upon the floor. "My darling!" she cried. Her winsome, childish beauty almost disarmed him, and surely he read once again the old love-light in her eyes.

Instantly he thought his friend had been mistaken – it could not have been his wife whom he had seen.

"Ruby," he began, speaking in the old, tender accents. "You were not up in town while I was in Scotland, were you, dear?"

Her face instantly paled to ashy whiteness, while her eyes drooped guiltily beneath his steady gaze.

A long, terrible pause followed. Ruby stood, clutching convulsively at the arm of her chair, but she made no attempt to clear herself.

In death-like silence, Stanley turned and flung himself from the room.

That night, the maid was busy brushing out her mistress's hair, when a tap sounded at the door, followed by Stanley's entrance.

"I have come," he said in measured tones, when the maid had quitted the room, "to acquaint you with the fact that I am joining a yachting expedition. I shall not return to England, probably for many months."

"Many months!" echoed his wife in faltering voice, her mouth quivering like a child's.

"Yes," he retorted sharply, for he instinctively felt that her thoughts were not of him at that moment.

"Stanley," she murmured, gently touching his arm, "there is something that – that I want to tell you before you go."

But he shook her off roughly.

"It is too late," he cried bitterly. "I have no time to listen to you now. I must catch the night express to London."

She shrank back like one who had received a blinding blow, the pain at her heart too deep for words. Her head sank upon her breast.

Something like pity touched Stanley, as he saw her droop like a broken lily. How beautiful she looked in her loose white robe, over which fell her luxuriant tresses.

For more than a second, he stood wavering, almost regretting his hasty decision; but he was not a man to change his mind.

With a hurried word of farewell, he quitted the room, but the memory of her shrinking form and drooping head haunted him for many a day.

Long months had come and gone, and the exquisite beauty of summertime had flown and gone.

The dismal landscape beyond stretched out, dark and dreary, before Ruby's wistful gaze.

By the curtained window she stood, lost in thought. A slip of paper lay idly in her listless fingers. It was a full receipt for that money she had borrowed for her brother. How she had saved, all through those long months, in order to pay off the wretched debt, and now it was paid – and just in time. Something of its crushing weight had been lifted from her heart, yet her heart still was sore and aching.

As she leaned thus beside the closed casement, she clasped her hands together in mute appeal.

"I know I shall not be happy," she murmured, "until I have confessed all. Perhaps Stanley will understand and forgive. Oh, if he only knew how miserable I have been!"

As she mused, the silent tears trickled down her cheeks, but she so often wept now that she had ceased to wonder at her own weakness.

"I did not want to deceive him; indeed I did not," she sighed. "I must write at once."

Drawing her blotter toward her, she sat beside the window and began a confession, her fingers trembling as she wrote the words. She did not spare herself. She told of her brother's visit, and how she had consented to do what she knew would displease her husband.

Bitterly she blamed herself, and earnestly implored his forgiveness. "If not for my own sake," she wrote, "let me plead, dear Stanley, on behalf of the little baby whom God is giving to us, for our little child's sweet sake. I wanted so to have told you this that last evening, ere you left home, but you said you were in a hurry, and had not time to listen. Don't you remember, dear?"

Here she paused, and the page became wet and blurred by many a tear. She rested a hand on her belly – but now a great pain came on her, so sudden and fast that she was afraid. She breathed deeply until it abated.

Ah, there was much which one might read between the lines in this letter. Ruby's firm writing was at fault for once; the iron had entered her soul, and the words were wrung from a crushed and lonely heart.

Nor had she finished yet, but Ruby was very weary. Leaning upon the table, she rested her tired head upon her hands and wondered, as she had so often done before, if it would all come right again, this tangled life of hers. Would the glad old days, so full of joy and sweetness, dawn once more? Yes, perhaps they might. Perhaps this little baby would help make everything right. This was the hope which kept her from giving way.

The chilliness of the December day was forgotten as she sat and dreamed, with all the tenderness of her loving nature, about the future. But once again, old Bridget came to disturb her, bearing a message from her absent husband, saying that he had returned to England at last.

Oh, how sweet was the news. Ruby's pensive lips smiled again, and the sad eyes grew radiant with the old, tender lights of deep, true love.

The pain came again. When it abated, she called, "Bridget … please, Bridget, send for the midwife."

A day passed. And, ere that winter's day had closed, there was born, to the noble house of Cleveland, a son and heir.

The cold December sun shone into the luxurious chamber where the young mother lay, its feeble rays touching with lingering caresses her bright hair, tossed carelessly back upon the pillows.

Presently the sleeper stirred and opened her eyes. "Was it only a dream?" she murmured. "I thought Stanley was with me."

Then, more fully awake, she turned eagerly towards her old nurse, who sat beside her.

"Hasn't he come?" she asked, almost piteously.

"Not as yet, Alana," soothed the woman gently. "Maybes as them trains is delayed, same as our old Kerry ones was oft!"

But the disappointed wife turned her face away again.

"You said that yesterday, Bridget," she faltered, her breath catching. "I wanted so to show him our boy, but perhaps…"

A little choking sob finished the broken sentence, and the eyelids closed wearily upon the glittering teardrops.

"Do not waken me, nurse," she sighed dreamily, "if I sleep again, because God gives me such happy visions, and it is so hard to awake and find Stanley gone, and that it was all but a dream – only a sweet, fleeting, empty dream, and nothing more."

The sun was now sinking to rest, and the frosty sky was flushed with crimson.

Now Stanley Cleveland neared his beautiful ancestral home. Already he could see its high turrets standing out boldly against the warmly-tinted sky.

For a moment, he checked the impatience of his horse and allowed the reins to slacken and fall upon its neck. A smile lit up his handsome face, for he was thinking of his fair young wife. Soon she would nestle on his breast, and the past – the horrible, bitter past – would be forever forgotten.

True, it had been some days since his arrival in London, but he had tarried there, against his will, afraid that Ruby would guess how keenly he had missed her all these months, yearning for a glimpse of her sweet face.

But a great change in his attitude had been wrought by an interview with Jervis that day, who, in a penitent mood, confessed to Stanley the whole tale of how he had persuaded his sister to accompany him to London the very day after his departure for the Scottish lakes and obtain money from a "lender" in order to save him from disgrace and prison.

In a second, Stanley understood it all – his poor wife's silence, her many tears.

Upbraiding himself most bitterly for judging his wife so cruelly, he took the very next train for Cloverdale, grumbling each mile at its slowness. How glad Ruby would be to know that all his miserable jealousy was at an end. Never again must the faintest shadow fall between their reunited hearts.

He smiled again, more tenderly than before, almost fancying in his rapture that he could feel her in his arms, and the soft touch of her brown hair against his cheek.

He passed unnoticed through the front entrance, and approached the house. But how strangely deserted it all looked. The blinds were drawn. What could it mean? Had she grown weary of the solitude, and gone from home?

Tossing the reins from his trembling hand, he sprang up the wide steps. His loud ring seemed to peal and echo through the gloom and silence of the darkened mansion.

A manservant threw open the door. His frightened face grew white as he met his master's questioning gaze.

"Speak! Speak!" cried Cleveland impatiently.

But, at that moment, a woman's wrinkled hand was laid upon his arm. To his astonishment, he beheld his wife's old Irish nurse, her face swollen from recent weeping, who silently motioned him to follow her into the house.

Half dazed, like one suddenly deprived of sight, he stumbled after her retreating figure. In solemn silence she led the way to the pretty morning-room, Ruby's favorite apartment.

"Oh! Sir," burst forth the old woman, with a choking sob, as she wiped her red eyes with the corner of her checkered apron. "She did grieve sore, as you didn't come, an' she wearied her poor strength out in watching for you. But the poor lamb's last words were of you – you and the little master. Dear, dear! An' to think as he have no mother now!"

"I don't understand," Cleveland said.

But a mewling cry came from the bed. Dumbly, he went there. There was a midwife holding a small bundle – a baby, newly born.

And there lay his wife, her face paler than he had ever seen it, sleeping peacefully – for eternity.

Reeling back as though stunned by a blow, Stanley Cleveland sank upon a chair, his head falling forward upon the table. No sound escaped his closed, bloodless lips.

In an agony of pain, he stretched forth his hands. They touched something – but it was only his wife's unfinished letter to him, blurred and blotted by many a tearstain.

With a long-drawn sigh of relief, Dewla laid down her pen. Once she'd read the manuscript carefully through, she folded the crackling sheets and placed them in an envelope.

Where should she send her precious tale? This was the burning question of the moment.

At length, as she pondered over the various names of the many magazines of the day, she made a choice – one which Hugh read – and, taking up her pen again, she wrote the address in clear, firm characters.

CHAPTER V

IT was St. Patrick's Day. Much to Dewla's delight, a little box arrived by the early post containing shamrocks all the way from Claisín, sent by her old nurse, Hannah.

With childish glee, she immediately fastened a large piece in her own frock, quite proud of her emblematical badge. The feminine members of the Smith family deigned to accept a piece each, because, as they explained, "It was quite the fashion this year, thanks to Royal favor." True to form, Mrs. Jonathan managed to "accidently" drop hers in the fire almost immediately.

Hugh was the only one unadorned with Ireland's simple weed. Dewla had felt shy of presenting it to him, for, of late, she fancied that Hugh no longer cared for anything Irish – even her own self.

It was a bitterly painful thought, and one which wounded her to the quick, causing many long hours of silent suffering. More than once that morning, she had come timidly towards him, armed with the choicest piece she could find, but a glance at his cold face dispelled her courage and she shrank away again.

She did not know – did not dream – that, all the while, he was wishing for her to offer it, only too proud to ask it of her himself.

Hugh returned from his office earlier than the usual hour. He looked pale and tired. "Had a beastly headache," he said, "and my throat is bothering me a bit."

Mrs. Jonathan fussed a good deal over him, suggesting all kinds of remedies, but he did not seem inclined to follow any of her many recipes.

Dewla grew very anxious as the day drew to a close. She had never seen her husband ill before. He drooped on the davenport, with little inclination to join in their discussion. She longed to soothe and comfort him, but his mother and sisters thrust her, as it were, on one side, and she lacked the nerve to remonstrate. Not that she was lacking in courage, but a sort of newborn shyness held her aloof.

"He does not need me," she thought sadly as she left the little group and wended her way upstairs to her own room. Kneeling beside the smoldering fire, she spread out her hands towards the feeble blaze, for the night was bitterly cold, and snow had fallen at intervals during the evening. Already the housetops outside her window were white once more.

Dewla felt very miserable. A strange foreboding of sorrow possessed her mind. What if Hugh should be very ill – dangerously ill – like Charlie! With a little stifled sob, her head sank upon her breast, touching the green spray of shamrock nestling there.

Hugh had followed his wife from the room, his quick eyes noticing the anxiety depicted on her face, for hers was a countenance which expressed, as plainly as words could, the pain or pleasure of her heart. With a thrill of surprise, he realized that he meant something to her yet.

Once again he stood unseen by her as she knelt upon the soft rug. How beautiful she looked in her simple white robe, unadorned save for the tuft of emerald green close to her delicate neck.

"Dewie," he said very softly. He came close to where she was and lay his hand upon her coil of nut-brown hair.

With a little start, she looked up wonderingly. It was so long since he had called her by the old pet-name of her childhood days. He was quick to see the teardrops trembling on her long lashes.

"You mustn't worry," he went on, drawing a chair to her side. "I dare say I shall feel better in the morning, but my throat is horribly sore."

"I wish I could do something to cure it," she whispered, with the sound of a sob in her voice, and she leaned her head against his knee.

With a sudden impulse, he stooped down, and, taking her face between his hands, kissed the quivering lips again and again.

"There!" he cried remorsefully. "I shouldn't have done that, for perhaps you'll get the bad throat; then, what should I do?"

But she only laughed in the great gladness of her heart – the first real laugh for many a long day. It did Hugh good to hear the merry sound again.

"Well, this is a great day for Ireland," he went on, trying to forget the pain of his throat. "Why, the 'Emerald Isle' is the topic above all others. From the Mansion House in London, the green flag emblazoned with the Irish harp floated today, for the first time in civic history. I think a bright future has dawned for your well-beloved country, Dewie."

"I am so thankful – so glad," was all she could say, but it was not altogether of Ireland that she thought just then, but of herself and him.

"Half the people I met today were decorated with shamrocks, and – why, I hadn't even one leaf!"

"Oh, Hugh, how sorry I am," she cried in consternation. Then, taking the spray from her own dress, she fastened it with trembling fingers in the buttonhole of his coat.

He stooped and touched the little fumbling hand. Never had Dewla felt so glad and happy. Surely, the long, bitter past was gone forever – only sunshine awaited them in the future.

With smiling gravity, Hugh surveyed her decoration. "What a pretty little leaf it has," he said thoughtfully.

"Yes, I just love it. In one of his charming ballads, Moore tells us the trifoliate represents 'Love, valor, and wit.'"

"And I think he was right," agreed Hugh, with considerable warmth. "All the world is talking today of the brave sons of Erin, who have so nobly lain down their lives in South Africa for their Queen and freedom."

"Oh, Hugh, how glad I am to hear you talk like this." Tears of pure joy rolled down her cheeks and fell upon her hands, now clasped upon his knee.

At that moment, a heavy step was heard and a rustling of silk. Then Mrs. Jonathan came bustling in.

Dewla drew back into the shadows.

"Where's this naughty boy of mine?" panted the great lady, almost breathless from the ascent upstairs. "I've come to hunt him off to bed – the best place for an invalid."

Hugh made some feeble remonstrance, for he was, in truth, feeling decidedly ill, but he did not want to leave Dewla's room.

"If you are not better in the morning, I'll send for Dr. Johnston." With this sort of threat, she sank upon a chair, gasping a little, for she was still out of breath from climbing the stairs.

Then her eyes, growing more accustomed to the dim firelight, spied Dewla for the first time.

"Dewla!" she scolded. "Why didn't you speak, child? You gave me quite a scare. In your white dress, you look just like a ghost! You should not frighten people so – it is bad for the nervous system. But then, of course, you cannot be expected to understand, as I believe Irish people are made of some kind of wrought iron, and never feel anything."

Hugh roused himself at this. "You are mistaken," he said in firm though hoarse tones. "There is no nation under the sun more considerate for the feelings of others than the people of the Emerald Isle. They are kindness itself."

Mrs. Jonathan rose with an affronted rustle. "I am *sure* you are in a high fever, Hugh, to be talking like this," she declared. "I wish Dewla would display some of this national consideration of which you boast so highly, and not keep you talking till midnight."

Then, gathering her train up clumsily in her left hand, she bustled off again, leaving Dewla and Hugh alone once more.

But the sweet, happy spell was broken. The great lady had swept in like a blighting frost, nipping and chilling the tender buds of joy.

After an awkward silence, Hugh rose. "I had better go to sleep," he said. "I fear that I have never felt so seedy before. Good night."

He left the room.

Dewla's tender nature was crushed, and her eyes dimmed with unshed tears.

CHAPTER VI

THE following morning found Hugh very ill indeed. His head ached to such a degree that he could not lift it from the pillow. A fever-flush burnt upon his cheek, and his eyes looked unusually bright.

In alarm, the family physician was summoned. When he had examined his patient, he drew Dewla from the sickroom.

"You must not remain," he said with decision. "I will send a nurse at once. Your husband has scarlet fever, I am afraid. In any case, it is wiser to run no risks."

Dewla's face paled.

"I am not afraid," she answered quickly. "I know something of nursing. I can be of use if you will only try me."

"But if you have never had it yourself, the chances are that you will only fall ill, too."

Dewla looked up with her dark, brave eyes. "Whatever the risk, I mean to stay at my husband's side."

The doctor shook his head. "I must see what Mrs. Jonathan has to say about that."

He was about to continue his journey down the stairs when Dewla sprang to stop him.

"Please," she cried, in quick, low tones, "allow me to have my way and remain. If you refer the question to my mother-in-law, she will only say 'No' at once."

In her anxiety to gain her point, she did not hear the rustling of silken skirts upon the landing. It was the great lady of the house approaching, and she heard Dewla's words.

"Very *dutiful* of you, my dear," she said, scornfully. "I am sure I feel highly flattered."

The doctor came to the rescue, for his young companion had started back, covered with confusion.

"It is very plucky of you to wish to remain in a fever room," he said gravely, taking Dewla's hand.

"Fever!" cried Mrs. Jonathan in dire dismay, echoing his words. "Surely Hugh is not so ill?"

"I am afraid he is, madam. As his fever may prove infectious, I recommend complete isolation from the rest of the family."

"Certainly, certainly!" returned the affrighted woman. "My daughters must be considered first. They are so nervous."

"Then, please allow me to help to nurse my husband," faltered Dewla, speaking only to the doctor. "I am not in the least frightened, and I know a good deal about the care of invalids, for my papa was ill so long. And Hugh and I were together last night, talking, so I might already have it. I may as well stay with him."

The doctor eyed her sharply, and she met his scrutiny without a quiver.

"I think you'll do," he said, bluntly. "Yes, Mrs. Jonathan, we'll let this foolish young person have her way, and if she gets knocked down herself, why, she can't blame us, can she?"

But the great lady was departing hurriedly in search of her daughters, to convey to them the alarming intelligence of Hugh's serious illness.

The most profound dismay soon prevailed in Trafalgar House – a perfect panic, in fact. Mistresses and maids alike were greatly alarmed.

Dewla returned at once to her sick husband's room, thankful at heart for being allowed to remain at her post. She was also pleased at finally being allowed to stay in her husband's room with him, for when they had arrived home from their honeymoon, Mrs. Jonathan had seen to it that they slept in separate apartments.

Hugh was very, very ill, and he could not bear the slightest sound. His wife's restful presence by his couch seemed to soothe him. He smiled a little at her from under her covers, his eyes looking weak and tired, and he took her little hand in his burning-hot hand.

"Don't leave me, Dewie," he begged in a low, faint whisper, unconscious of the risk she ran.

"I will not leave you," she said softly in reply, smiling because he had called her by the old name, "Dewie."

How long the day seemed. Yet those watching hours were very precious to Dewla. As she sat beside her husband, while he sank now and again into fitful, feverish slumbers, she began to realize how unutterably dear and precious he had grown to her. How she loved him, none but her own heart knew.

A cold, wintry blast swept through the stunted, leafless trees outside, and moaned dismally around the house. As she listened to the mournful sound, she shivered, for it brought back the old tales from her childhood – of banshees, whose wailing cry was always a prediction of coming sorrow to those who heard the sound.

With an effort, she put such superstitions from her mind. Drawing her Bible to her side, she softly turned the pages over, looking for needed comfort there.

With a deep sigh, Hugh presently opened his eyes. They rested on Dewla's wistful face. He smiled faintly.

"Little wife," he said, "read me something. I like the sound of your voice – no one else speaks so softly."

Dewla hesitated, then she asked timidly, "May I read from my Bible – just as I used to read for Father?"

"Certainly," he replied, "it is the sound I want, more than anything."

Thus encouraged, she began to read one of her favorite Psalms – the 103rd. How beautiful the sacred words seemed just now.

The sick man was touched by their preciousness. "Thank you, Dewie," he murmured. "I liked both – the words and your voice."

At last he slumbered again, not awaking even at the entrance of the nurse.

Dewla, at her post, watching and waiting, had ample time for reflection.

In the evening, when the doctor looked in again, he found but little change in his patient's condition. He looked grave, though he said but little.

Much against her will, he insisted that Dewla must have an undisturbed night's rest. In vain she protested and pleaded – but he would not listen.

"We don't want two patients on our hands, instead of one," he returned, speaking as gruffly as he could.

Seeing that resistance was useless, she gave in at length, only on conditions that she might be allowed to watch in the sickroom on the following night.

Next day, Dewla found herself entirely cut off from the rest of the family – which, she had to admit to herself, was so much more peaceful. Only Mrs. Jonathan, whose anxiety on her son's behalf got the better of her fears, communicated with her at a safe distance, but she did not stay long, much to Dewla's relief.

Hugh's temperature began to rise rapidly towards night. The nurse, fearing perhaps that delirium might set in, begged to be allowed to remain with Dewla and share the night watch with her. Dewla would not listen to this.

"No," she said gently, "I rested last night and now feel quite fresh, but you look quite exhausted. Go and get some sleep; it will do you good."

Slowly the time crept by – the long, lonely hours of midnight. Hugh began to toss to and fro, and his sleep was broken.

Dewla came softly to his side. Seeing in the dim light that his eyes were open, she said softly, "Hugh, dear."

He turned towards her fiercely. "Go away," he cried. "Why will you stay here, when you know none of us want you?"

Dewla gasped. She had never seen anyone delirious before, and did not know that he was not accountable for his words. Such a thought never entered her head.

Trembling so that she scarce could speak, she whispered soothingly, "Hugh, I am Dewla – your wife, Dewla."

He turned from her sharply. "I do not want you; once again I tell you so. I only want Bella."

With a low moan, she sank upon the chair beside his bed.

"Yes, go away, you! and send me Bella. I love Bella. But you – why, I hate you. Didn't you know it? Oh! yes, you do know it. Go away, I say! Don't you hear me?"

Dewla did not stir; she had no strength left. Motionless, she crouched, half-hidden by the silken draperies, too miserable for words.

Again Hugh's voice fell upon her ears.

"Bella, Bella," he moaned, turning his head from side to side on the pillow, "why do you not come when I call you?"

Covering her face with her hands, Dewla remained rooted to the spot. It was true, then, the terrible thing which she had feared. Mrs. Jonathan's many taunts came crowding back with cruel force.

She saw it all as clear as daylight – why her presence was so unwelcome at Trafalgar House. Hugh had loved the fair Bella long before he met her, and she – in ignorance though it was – had separated them forever.

Oh, that she had only the power to undo the wrong! She loved her husband so well, that she was willing and ready to sacrifice herself and happiness for his sake. What would she not willingly give to set him free once more?

What a terrible mistake her marriage had been – that midnight ceremony, performed in haste.

"Oh, Father!" her heart cried out, in its bitter pain, "why did you seek to bind me thus to a stranger – one who had naught of love left to give? And yet, Hugh would not disappoint your wishes. In the nobleness of his nature, he allowed himself to be sacrificed, in order that you may be pleased – you, the dearly-beloved friend of his father's boyhood. Oh, Hugh! how good you were to do all this for him and me."

Hugh whispered words she could not understand, now muttering in his delirium, and her hands trembled as she lay a cool compress on his brow.

CHAPTER VII

DEWLA had no more night-watches, for the arrival of the second nurse prevented that. Only in the daytime was she allowed to remain in Hugh's room. But the memory of Hugh's strange words stuck in her breast and rankled there. Day and night, they haunted her.

The patient was now improving rapidly; each day he was feeling better.

The three Miss Smiths had gone away from home in case of infection. Only their mother remained behind. When the first shock of her son's illness had worn off, she was less cautious and allowed Dewla more freedom through the house, particularly after the doctor had pronounced the case not scarlet fever, as at first anticipated.

One evening, Dewla came down to fetch something forgotten by the nurse in the breakfast room.

As she neared the door, which stood ajar, she overheard Mrs. Jonathan saying in a loud, excited voice, "Why, my dear Bella! That Kerry marriage has proved most disastrous to Hugh's happiness. He is not the same. Would to Heaven he had never gone to those beggarly people in Ireland, and got entrapped into such a low connection!"

Dewla had paused, shocked by what she heard – unconscious, for the moment, that the conversation was not intended for her ears.

"But," argued a girl's voice, "does he not care very much for his wife?"

"No," retorted the angry woman. "His fancy was caught by a fresh face, but now the novelty has worn off. To be quite frank, I don't think he ever loved her."

Now, the cruel words that Mrs. Jonathan said burst upon Dewla's mind. With a low, bitter cry, she fled, forgetting the errand on which she had come.

On the other side of the door, Bella started guiltily on hearing the faint cry and the sound of retreating footsteps.

"Can she have heard?" gasped the girl, gazing anxiously into her companion's face.

Mrs. Jonathan merely laughed. "What if she has?" she retorted. "Serves her right. It will teach her not to play the eavesdropper in my house again. I don't know what it is about that girl, but she makes me feel perfectly savage."

"And yet," returned the visitor, "she seems so sweet and lovable. I often wonder how it is you are not all fonder of her."

Mrs. Jonathan shrugged her shoulders. "We won't discuss the subject any further, Bella. I never liked the idea of my son taking to himself an Irish wife."

"But Mrs. Jonathan," persisted Miss Sedley, "that surely is prejudice. All the world is raving over Ireland just now. The wild enthusiasm on St. Patrick's Day made me quite envious, and I really longed to be a real daughter of the land of bravery and shamrocks."

"Why, I do believe you like *Hugh's wife*," declared Mrs. Jonathan, with considerable stress on the last two words.

Bella Sedley colored, but she had known before now that her weakness for Hugh was well known both to his mother and sisters.

"Yes," she answered slowly, "from the first I liked your daughter-in-law's face. I couldn't help it, somehow, though I had fully made up my mind to thoroughly dislike her. I tried my best to do so, but all to no avail. Mrs. Jonathan, forgive me if I offend you, but I do believe she has a good heart."

The great lady shook her head impatiently. "I never could endure the Irish," she repeated again as though in self-defense.

"But, surely, the Queen herself is setting her seal to the acknowledgment of their magnificent valor and genuine bravery. Ireland will be quite the fashion this season. After Her Majesty's visit, it will be the most popular resort for the summer. I am glad she is going over, because the Irish must naturally have felt keenly her long absence from their beautiful island."

Mrs. Jonathan frowned. "You talk exactly like Dewla," she declared.

"When are the girls returning?" inquired Bella, anxious to change the topic, for she saw plainly that the lady of the house was determined to be unpleasant about it.

"They did not say. I wrote and told them that the scare of fever was over, but they seem in no hurry to come back. I wish they would, of course, because I miss them very much."

"If I should be of any use, pray say so. I will gladly come and spend a week or so with you. Mother can spare me quite well, and I should like it."

Mrs. Jonathan jumped at the idea. She was already heartily tired of her own company, and gladly hailed any change in the forced monotony of her life.

"It is most kind," Mrs. Jonathan began warmly. "I have no one to drive out with me in the afternoons. Dewla is always hiding in the sickroom. At any rate, I would prefer a lonely drive to being in her society. She is always so silent and moping that it gives one the blues."

"Then is it settled, Mrs. Jonathan?" asked Bella, rising.

"Well," mused the great lady, meditatively. "This is the twenty-third, is it not? So, can you come on the twenty-fifth?"

"Certainly. I needn't bring much baggage, I suppose?"

"It is very kind of you, Bella," returned Mrs. Jonathan gratefully. "I am sure Hugh will be very glad for someone to chat with while he is convalescent. I expect, if the truth were known, he finds Dewla particularly dull."

Bella looked surprised. "Why, it was only last evening Mr. De Vere was at our house saying how charming Mrs. Hugh was, and how well she could talk."

"There, there! My dear," retorted the old lady, "you certainly seem determined to champion Dewla today, so it's no use my saying anything more. I do not approve of those tete-a-tetes she and Mr. De Vere hold together. She simply drags him into arguments about St. Patrick and all such rubbish."

Bella laughed. "I think it is a little dangerous just now – even in England – to couple that great saint with 'rubbish,' dear Mrs. Jonathan. We are all growing so suddenly loyal to the land of shamrock."

"Not much!" retorted she, stiffly. "I hate to read the papers nowadays, as they are so full of Ireland. Why can't people leave it in obscurity a little longer, I wonder?"

"I suppose 'tis a case of 'whom the king delighteth to honor,' only in this case, it is a queen." Miss Sedley rose to depart, pretending not to see Mrs. Jonathan's gigantic frown. "Then, I'll come on Sunday evening – that is settled, is it not?"

Mrs. Jonathan grudgingly assented, and Bella hurriedly escaped, feeling shaken, almost as if she'd fought a lion hand to hand.

CHAPTER VIII

AND Dewla – what of her?

In brokenhearted haste, she fled from the spot where she had overheard her mother-in-law declaring that Hugh no longer cared for her; that, indeed, their hasty marriage had been disastrous to her son's happiness. Reaching the privacy of her own room, she threw herself beside the bed, and hid her face in the counterpane.

What must she do? Was there no way in which she might loose the chain that bound Hugh to her? Could she not set him free – free to marry Bella Sedley?

At this last suggestion, she nearly cried aloud from the bitter pain at her heart. Hugh had become to her the dearest of all things in the wide, wide world. Everything else was as nothing, compared with his love.

Her head throbbed – seemed all on fire.

Rising, she threw open the casement so that the evening air might cool her heated brow. She looked out over the dreary landscape that forever greeted her eyes.

How terribly, at this moment, did she miss the soothing influence of her dear country home. Instead of the hoary, lichen-grown lilac trees, familiar to her from childhood, and the evergreens of the shrubbery, her eyes were assailed by a dull row of blackened roofs and grim chimneypots, monotonous. Instead of the sweet birds twittering on the boughs outside her window, and filling the still woodland with thrilling notes of evensong, she heard now the ceaseless roar of distant traffic in the busy district, broken by an occasional shrill and long whistle from the Hanley train station.

What would she not give, at this moment, for a walk beneath the giant trees on the lawn, which had spread their sheltering branches over many a past generation of O'Donoughs? Surely they would soothe the tumult of her breast.

"Why did I ever leave?" she moaned. "And yet – and yet I loved – I love still my husband too dearly to want to obliterate the few months of our wedded life from my memory. Oh, Hugh! I would not, even if I could, recall the past – the past without you."

Presently a tap sounded on the door. Hastily wiping her eyes, Dewla said, "Come in."

It was the nurse, to say Mr. Smith was wondering why she had remained away so long, and was asking for her.

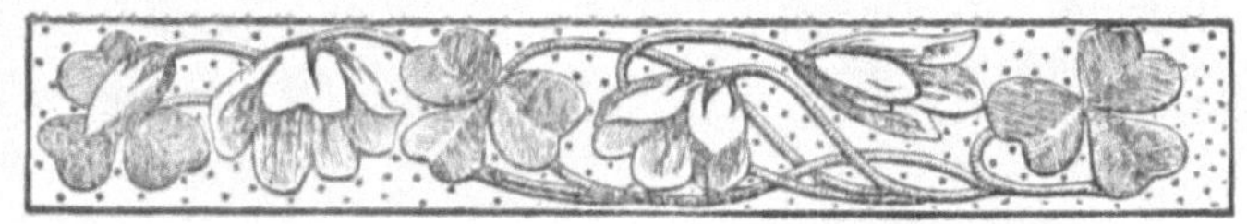

"Dewla, my dear," Mrs. Jonathan was saying, in her usual bland tones, "I have a pleasant surprise for you."

Dewla tensed. Never had a surprise from this woman ever been 'pleasant.'

"Bella Sedley is coming to our house to help to amuse Hugh, now that he is better! Isn't that lovely news?"

Dewla seemed hardly to understand at first.

"She is coming to *stay* here, I mean," continued the great lady with a chilly smile. "You see, it is so dull without any of the girls at home."

"To … stay?" murmured Dewla, slowly. Her face had grown pale, and her lips trembled.

"Why, of course she is! Why not?" Mrs. Jonathan said, feigning surprise. "Bella has always been very intimate here."

Dewla stood in silence, gazing before her in a vacant sort of way.

"It will be nice for Hugh to have her to talk to when he is better, for she is so bright," continued the same bland voice, "One needs brightness, as much as anything, in a sickroom. It is part of the cure, I believe, to have a merry face about."

And Dewla, painfully conscious that her own face was anything but gay, said not a word. With averted face, she stood as though glued to the floor, trembling in every limb like a leaf in a gale.

At length she spoke, and her voice had a strange, unnatural sound; even Mrs. Jonathan must have noticed this.

"When does she come?"

"Tomorrow evening," Mrs. Jonathan said in a cloying voice. "Isn't it sweet of her? Hugh will be pleased. You know what friends they were *once*." The great lady sighed, as though to imply that some sudden misfortune had occurred to break that friendship suddenly.

Dewla clasped her hands together tightly. *Don't speak,* she urged herself as she fought to curb her tongue. She had always been obedient to her dear father – had always obeyed him. She had done the same for Mrs. Jonathan, though her words and happy cruelty had rankled deeply.

But now she turned on the great lady.

"Your son married *me*, not Bella," she said quietly. "So what are you playing at here? Are you trying to play matchmaker between Hugh and Bella now? Is that it?"

Mrs. Jonathan's eyes went wide as if Dewla had slapped her across the face. Her mouth flapped once – twice –

And then she shrieked.

"You little hoyden! How dare you talk back!"

"How dare you try to make your son be unfaithful to his own Christian wife," Dewla cried. "Are you going to drive him to the magistrate and force him to get a *divorce* just so your will can be satisfied?"

Mrs. Jonathan clenched her teeth, her face flushing. "A divorce! How dare you! How dare you insinuate –"

"I am not insinuating. I can see how it delights you to dash Bella's name in my face."

The great lady grabbed Dewla by the arms and shook her. "You have no right to say any of those scandalous things. How *dare* you—"

Dewla wrenched away. "I have a perfect right to defend my marriage against a presumptuous toad with a black heart, who smiles as she torments a girl who is lost and alone in a strange country!"

"I told Hugh not to marry a wild Irish girl," Mrs. Jonathan cried. "It is no wonder, now, is it, that I should call on Miss Sedley to install her in your place in Hugh's sickroom? She is woman more fitted to comfort and cheer my son, for you are too unstable, you little savage."

Little did Mrs. Jonathan guess – or care – what strange thoughts and plans were passing through her companion's brain as she stood there, trembling all over, unable to fight back.

Dewla turned on her heel and fled the room, feeling utterly broken.

With quick, weary steps, she began to ascend the great, wide staircase. The carved figures looked upon her with grave, calm dignity, and her own chiseled face was hardly less white than theirs.

She had never fought anybody thus in her life – had never needed to, for nobody had galled her and crushed her so assiduously as that woman and her daughters had.

Standing upon the first landing, Dewla looked about her with a burning light in her dark eyes. Wealth and luxury were displayed on every hand – all that money could purchase.

"No wonder," she said to herself, "that Hugh thought us poor and shabby at Claisín. Yet to me it was home, sweet home. This place has never been that — never home, nor sweet – to me. There is not a whit of love in this terrible place. Only cruelty and hatred."

The hurtful words that Hugh had said to her on his bed of sickness, the daily taunts from his sisters, and the smile in her mother-in-law's eyes every time she said something to Dewla to cut her – all of these came back to her now.

Dewla had come to this grand, stern house, a stranger in a strange country, hoping to find love from her new family. They had merely closed their hearts and smiled as they watched her smile melt away, day after day.

She was finished.

Upon entering her room, Dewla shut and locked the door. Opening a drawer, she drew out a black gown – the one she had worn on the day she first arrived at Trafalgar House. Finding her purse, she carefully counted its contents – twenty pounds, all told. Here was the little Bible she loved, and a few other things. These she placed together on a side table. None of the costly jewels which Hugh had bought her did she touch. Everything else remained just as usual. Her beautiful dresses and hats did not even receive a second glance from her.

"Tomorrow evening, Bella is coming." Dewla sat down upon the window-seat, anguish upon her face.

"I could never stay, with these cruel women always harping at me – and –" with a catch in her breath, "Hugh will not miss me. I am thankful he is better. I could hardly have torn myself away otherwise. But I know it is wiser to go. Better for him, and me."

At this, she broke down, and sobbed aloud.

"He has been so nice again, just lately. I was so happy until that night when he spoke of Bella, because alas! I hoped – hoped that he loved me. But no. He only pities me. And his mother only poisons his mind against me."

For a moment she stood thus, helpless and grieving.

The long, cold March day was drawing to a close. Evening had come.

Looking out upon the deepening twilight, Dewla sighed. "At this time tomorrow, I shall be far away, going home. God will help me. There is no one else – no one else who knows all, and pities me, as He does."

CHAPTER IX

SUNDAY morning dawned. Needless to say, Dewla had spent a sleepless night. Terrors of the great, unknown world filled her breast, and banished rest from her eyes.

Exhausted, she came downstairs to find that a letter awaited her on the breakfast table. Another time, the sight of her cousin's familiar writing would have filled her with joy. Today, she felt only a dulled sense of utter indifference, as though her heart were dead to all the world, buried in frost.

Of course, Mrs. Jonathan sat across from her at the table, staring at Dewla with her nose wrinkled as if she smelled something unpleasant.

Dewla slowly broke the seal, and began to read the closely-penned page. But even then she scarce took in a word. All the time, her heart was crying out in anguish: "I am going to leave Hugh today, and may never see him again."

Even with Charlie's tenderly-worded note before her eyes, her brain refused to comprehend its meaning. In vain she strove to collect her scattered senses, but she could think of nothing, save this only: "I am leaving, Hugh, because I love you so. Alas! If only you knew how much I love you."

Unconscious of the flying moments, she sat there, grasping the letter in her hand, caring not that Mrs. Jonathan's cold eyes, from where her mother-in-law sat opposite, were regarding her with a suspicious glitter, so wrapped in her thoughts was she.

Her breakfast still lay untasted. White and trembling, she sat in her usual place, only a ghost of the bonny bride who had come to Trafalgar House some months before, yearning for a mother's welcome and a mother's love.

This comparison did not escape the great lady's cruel eye. For the first time today she remarked the terrible change in her daughter-in-law's appearance.

"Dewla," she said, abruptly, "are you not well?"

The girl started, a flush spreading over her face. "I am well, thank you," she answered just as coldly.

"Then, pray put aside that seemingly enchanting epistle, and attend to your food. You wild Irish people are so wasteful."

Hardly knowing what she was doing, Dewla folded the unread note and replaced it in the envelope. It was a very poor attempt she made at having breakfast; for each morsel seemed to stick in her throat. At length she gave up, feeling that another crumb would choke her.

Before luncheon, Mrs. Jonathan had a little private conversation with her son, for she was certain that he was well enough by now to bear a little worry.

"Oh, Hugh, yesterday that terrible girl whom you call your bride – she had the gall to scream at me in the dining room," she moaned.

"Screamed at you?" Hugh said in disbelief, for he had never heard Dewla raise her voice.

"Oh! She did. She accused me of so many base things, oh my son! it still makes my heart beat fast to relive all the terrible things she accused me of. And then all she did during her breakfast was stare at that epistle from her dear cousin Charlie," the great lady carped. "To be sure, your wife's wild manner surprised me greatly. To my mind, there is but one solution to this mystery, which should be clear to anybody who has eyes. Your Irish girl is still in love with her gallant soldier-cousin. All she wants is to run away with him. To be quite honest, I wish she would."

Hugh listened in silence to all she had got to say, but the old, pained look returned in deeper measure to his brow. He sighed wearily. He had hoped since that night when Dewla tenderly placed the sweet little shamrock in his coat that her love was his. She had been so devoted during his weary days of illness. The nurse had told him how she had braved infection for his sake, even when he was thought to have scarlet fever. Her gentle voice, when she was reading her Bible to him – how it had soothed him in his pain! She had lingered ever by his bedside, even when he could see how exhausted she was.

But now, his mother's words dashed his dreams of happiness to the winds.

He rolled onto his side, burying his face in the pillow. "Poor little Dewie," he thought. "She loved her cousin first, and from the kindness of her heart, only married me to obey the dying wishes of her father."

Yet even this thought was bitter. He meant to treat his little wife with tenderness. Did she not love him after all?

"If I could but teach her to love me, even a little," he thought sadly. "Oh! what would I not give to win her affections."

With thoughts such as these, he listened for the sound of her light step – it was as music to his ears.

She came at length. With hungry eyes, Hugh scanned her pale, suffering face. Though the realization that she loved her cousin more broke his heart, far greater was his urge to soothe her in his pain. He could not bear to see her looking so sad and drooping. Even if she did not love him, he still loved her.

"Dewla," he murmured sadly, "how thin you have grown. Why, your hand is small as a child's. It is just like my selfishness, forcing you to be constantly indoors. No wonder that your cheeks are white. You look far more ill than I do – that I am sure of."

Dewla almost shrank from his touch. Her eyes drooped beneath his searching gaze, her heart beating almost to suffocation. With Hugh being so gentle with her, how hard it was to go away and leave him. It would be easier to go if he remained cold and distant.

Trembling, she sat down on the old seat beside the curtains, her face partly hidden in the shadow.

"You must go out more," he went on, trying to encourage her. "Now that spring has come, the country will look pretty again. When I am well enough, you and I shall have some nice long drives together, eh, Dewie?"

Her lips quivered; the color came and went upon her cheeks. Why was he so tender with her today – today of all days? Hot tears struggled for mastery, but she drove them back.

Hugh continued, eagerly, "This is the twenty-fifth of the month – I am sure I shall be quite fit again in a week. Johnston said I must have a little change at once. So what do you say, Dewie, to a run across to Dublin, and see Queen Victoria pay a royal visit to your beloved country? We could go together, you and me. You would like it, should you not?"

For a second, Dewla forgot herself in the wild surprise she felt at such a suggestion. Her whole face lit up with pleasure. Then, as suddenly, the light faded from her eyes, and she tried to stammer some faint words of thanks, thinking all the while of that other journey she was about to take.

"Ah! I thought you'd be sure to like it, Dewie," he said, smiling. "I never knew such an ardent, enthusiastic Paddy. Are all the Irish like you, I wonder?"

The kindness in his manner moved Dewla deeply. Bending down, she laid her cheek against his extended hand.

"I do not wonder at your patriotism, Dewie," he went on, softly. "All the world today is loud in its expressions of admiration over the bravery of the Irish regiments in South Africa. With such Irishmen as Wolseley, Roberts – the foremost of living British generals – also Kitchener, White, and French, the wonder is that there are no Irish Guards, and but few Irishmen in our artillery. I am hoping that our Queen's visit to Ireland may rectify this. It is only lately I have studied the question deeply; but now I know what Irish soldiers have been – not today only, but in the past. In the ranks of France, they astounded George II at Dettingen, and turned the scale of fate at Fontenoy. In the ranks of England, they have been the bravest of the brave, from the day of Vimiera to the day of Elandslaagte."

Dewla listened with mingled feelings. It warmed her heart to hear him talk thus of her beloved countrymen. But her heart was too heavy to feel altogether glad, as she might have done another time.

In silence she sat there, trying hard to forget the future, attempting to enjoy those few happy moments while they lasted, and they were still together.

Hugh, wondering at her long musings, suddenly thought of the letter that his mother had spoken of. Was this the reason of her continued silence? The suggestion smote upon his heart, and pained him deeply.

"Dewla," he said in an altered voice, "you did not tell me of Charlie's letter."

She started – not at his question, it is true, but the change in his manner. It was the old, cold tone once more. Her sweet dream of peace was broken.

"I heard from him this morning," she faltered, seeing that Hugh waited for her to speak. How strangely he was watching her. She trembled beneath the searching glances of his keen blue eyes, and the color rushed to her brow and neck.

"What did he say?" inquired the same cool tone, slowly and with deliberate clearness, which contrasted strangely with her faltering speech.

"He said—" she began absently, for she was puzzling in her mind at the sudden alteration of her husband's manner, "that – Oh! I don't know really, for I haven't read it yet."

Hugh Smith's lip curled. Had not his mother told him of Dewla's lengthened perusal of this same letter?

"Curious, that," he retorted, with all the bitterness of his nature roused, "considering your cousinly interest towards him!"

Dewla lifted her startled eyes to his. She had never heard his voice so harsh – it cut her to the very quick.

With unconcealed scorn, he turned his head away.

The long-repelled teardrops gathered afresh on Dewla's lashes, and fell unheeded upon the folds of her frock.

She was sure his mother had talked to him earlier and, drop by drop, had poisoned his mind against her.

Hugh never looked towards her again. In stolid silence, he turned his eyes the other way. After some time, he fell asleep, and his face – sullen, suspicious – softened into the loving face that made her heart ache.

The day was beginning to wane; the first faint shadows of eventide began to gather.

With a kind of gasp, Dewla jumped to her feet. "Miss Sedley will be coming soon," she whispered, "and I must be gone."

Yet still she stayed, half-hidden by the silken drapery, looking upon Hugh as he lay sleeping there. Never had she suffered more than now, when the moment for parting had come. She was so unwilling – almost powerless – to tear herself away.

How still it was, standing thus in the softening light. No sound was heard in the great house. All was quiet: outside, a Sabbath stillness reigned upon the busy streets – all was hushed and subdued, except for the sound of her husband's breathing.

But at length the peaceful silence was broken by Mrs. Jonathan's abrupt entrance.

"Dear me!" she cried, trying to regain her breath. "How dull you both seem. Dewla isn't very lively company in a sick-room, I'll be bound."

Hugh, who had awakened when his mother had crashed into the room, drew his hand wearily across his eyes. He could not endure his mother's slighting remarks directed towards his little wife. And yet he could not bring himself to defend Dewla.

Dewla's face was white as marble. Even her lips were colorless, but the uncertain light hid this from view, and the pain depicted on her fair young brow went unnoticed.

Hugh turned his eyes towards his wife, standing there in the shadow like a white-robed guardian spirit. Something in her attitude – the sorrowful droop of her shapely head, perhaps – impressed him a little. "Why is she so strangely quiet?" he wondered.

The sound of carriage wheels was heard approaching. Mrs. Jonathan bustled to the window, shoving past Dewla.

"It is dear Bella," she cried exultingly. "Now we shall have some sunshine in the house!" And, without further remark, she panted off to receive her guest with a flourish of trumpets.

A cold chill fastened about Dewla's heart. She must leave; the last moment had come. With great yearning, she bent forward until her cold, quivering lips touched her husband's forehead.

Surprised by her unusual demonstration of affection, Hugh took her face between his hands.

"What, tears!" he cried gaily. "Are you not glad to have Bella come? Silly child!" Still he did not release her, but held her fast.

With a little cry, Dewla's brown head sank upon his shoulder. "Please don't be angry with me," she begged, and broke down into sobbing, and was unable to say any more.

Startled by her sudden emotion, he tenderly stroked her soft hair and tried to soothe her as one might a child.

"My dear! You are quite worn out," he said. "I am glad Bella has come – very glad, indeed!" He spoke with quiet emphasis.

That immediately stopped her sobs. Dewla rose, and, with one final, long kiss, she fled, fearing lest her courage should give way at the end.

Into her own room she rushed and closed the door
Everything was ready for her proposed flight. She must
steal away in the dark, unnoticed by the household.

Would Hugh miss her? Would he be anxious?

Everything was ready for her proposed flight.

This thought compelled her to snatch up a pencil, and
she scribbled a few last words of farewell in a note to her
husband.

Dear, Dear Hugh,

I am going away because I know now you only married me out of pity. I love you so well that I cannot stay longer here. Please do not worry about me.

Your loving

DEWIE.

That was all. Dewla's writing was irregular and shaky-- not like her usual pretty hand.

Thrusting the little note into an envelope, she closed and directed it, then laid it upon her table for someone to find.

Kneeling beside her open window, she prayed long and earnestly that God would bless them both – Hugh and her.

Taking the little bag in which she had put away the few necessary things for her journey, she slipped out upon the landing with noiseless tread and down the dark back stairs. Because it was Sunday, nearly all of the maids were out, and thus Dewla escaped being seen.

Opening the side door, she hurried forth into the cold evening air, fearful lest Mrs. Jonathan might be in pursuit. But no; the place was silent and still – no one had noticed her going. Good.

The March wind blew sharp and keen. Dewla shivered, though her mind was so full of anguish that she was scarcely conscious of the bitter cold. With quick steps, she hurried on towards the station, carrying the small bag which contained all her worldly goods.

And at this very moment, if she could only have seen Hugh – stolid, unromantic Hugh – bending over something dark and withered that lay in his hand, and gazing fondly at it. If she could have seen this, would have changed her plans? For it was that same spray of shamrock which she herself had fastened in his coat.

Ah, if he loved so well and treasured her worthless gift, must he not love her too?

But she could not see, so she never knew.

"WHOM THE QUEEN HONORS" is the title of our next Story. It is an IRISH Story, written in a high-toned and unusually interesting style, by BIRDYE LATHAM HARTLAND; and contains an account of the QUEEN'S VISIT TO THE EMERALD ISLE.

WHOM THE QUEEN HONORS

A MAIDEN FLEES

Her husband's home no longer a home, Dewla flees into the dark streets of the city, not knowing where she will find refuge. But running away is better than watching her own mother-in-law bringing her husband's old sweetheart to take Dewla's place at his sickbed.

A HUSBAND DESPAIRS

Hugh doesn't understand why his wife left. It's not until a surprising ally comes forward with new information that he is forced to arrive at a realization – one that his mother is prepared to nip in the bud.

A NEW LIFE

As Dewla begins a new chapter in her life, writing stories, she needs to make a reckoning. Will she begin a new life, or will she find a way to return to her husband?

WHOM THE QUEEN HONORS is the final book in the clean and sweet Victorian romance series, The Shamrock Romances.

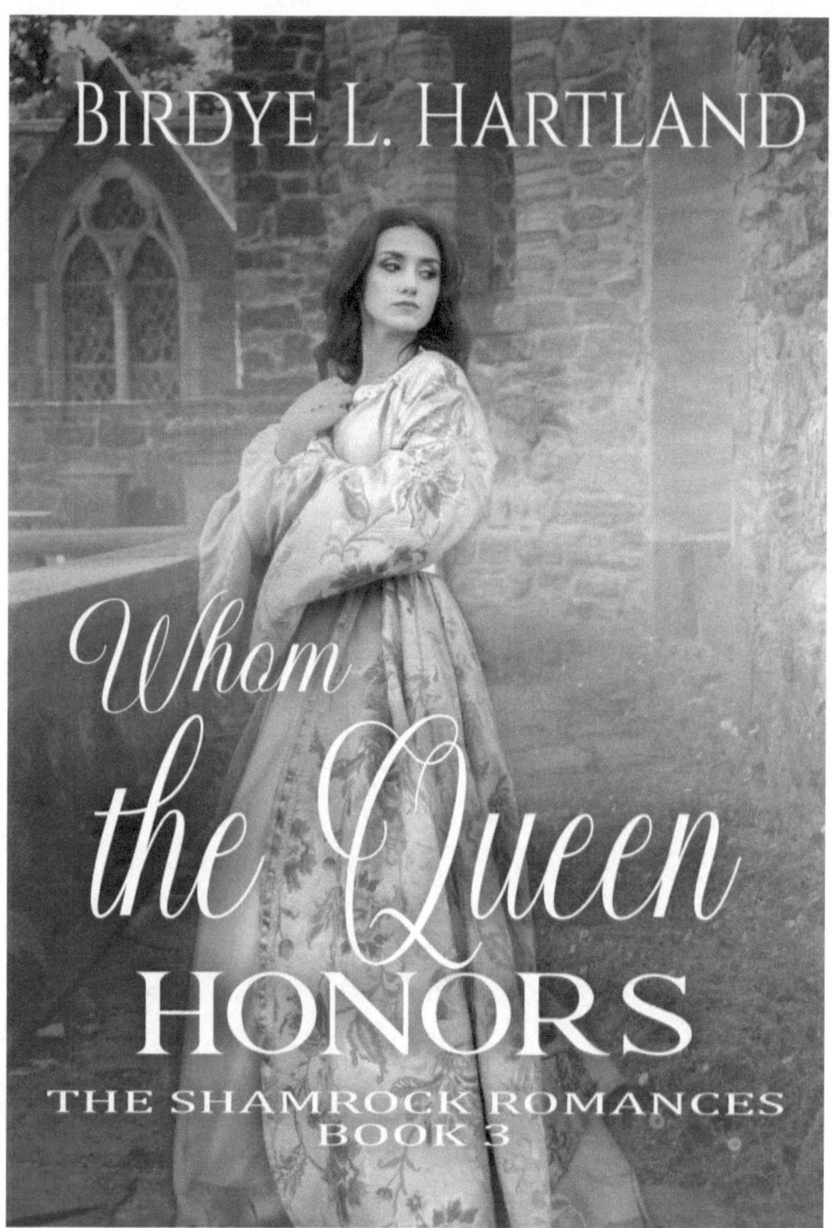
BIRDYE L. HARTLAND
Whom
the Queen
HONORS
THE SHAMROCK ROMANCES
BOOK 3

This good old story from Victorian England has now been tidied up and shaken into shape by our chipper Victorian book fiend and tireless editor, Eva Valentine. You can find her on Twitter, posting from some lonely and wind-swept tower from the moors, where she's been locked by some cruel fiend. Oh, I hope she has an internet connection out there!

Keep up with the latest serials from merry England by subscribing to our newsletter, SERIALLY YOURS. Follow Eva Valentine on Twitter at @VictorianReader, or on Tumblr!

92